本教材受江汉大学研究生处、江汉大学外国语学院教材建设项目出版资助

# 英美诗歌批评教程

刘晓燕　曾　莉　主编

华中科技大学出版社
http://www.hustp.com
中国·武汉

## 内容提要

本书为江汉大学研究生教材项目建设而编写,从众多英美诗歌批评文章中精选百余篇进行导读。本书以研究性思维贯穿始终,对晦涩难读的文学批评文章进行问题性引导,让学生能够基本掌握文学批评文章的研究思路与写作方法,培养学生的研究性思维,开拓其学术视野。除用作高校英语类研究生课程教学外,对于爱好文学的读者,本书也是一本优秀的参考读物。

### 图书在版编目(CIP)数据

英美诗歌批评教程/刘晓燕,曾莉主编. —武汉:华中科技大学出版社,2020.8
ISBN 978-7-5680-6485-9

Ⅰ. ①英… Ⅱ. ①刘… ②曾… Ⅲ. ①诗歌评论-英国 ②诗歌评论-美国
Ⅳ. ①I561.072 ②I712.072

中国版本图书馆CIP数据核字(2020)第144429号

### 英美诗歌批评教程
Yingmei Shige Piping Jiaocheng

刘晓燕 曾 莉 主编

策划编辑:刘 平
责任编辑:刘 凯
责任校对:张汇娟
封面设计:原色设计
责任监印:周治超

出版发行:华中科技大学出版社(中国·武汉)　　电话:(027)81321913
　　　　　武汉市东湖新技术开发区华工科技园　　邮编:430223
录　　排:华中科技大学出版社美编室
印　　刷:武汉开心印印务有限公司
开　　本:787mm×1092mm　1/16
印　　张:12
字　　数:227千字
版　　次:2020年8月第1版第1次印刷
定　　价:38.00元

本书若有印装质量问题,请向出版社营销中心调换
全国免费服务热线:400-6679-118　竭诚为您服务
版权所有　侵权必究

本教材系 2020 年湖北省教育厅教育科学规划项目"文化治理视野下在线课程中主体自治的方法与路径研究"(2020GB019),2020 年江汉大学青年教师专项教研项目"英美文学在线课程中转叙思维的应用模式与实践"(JyQ2020052)的阶段性成果之一

# Contents

**Part I　English Poets**

| | | |
|---|---|---|
| Chapter 1 | Geoffrey Chaucer | /003 |
| Chapter 2 | William Shakespeare | /009 |
| Chapter 3 | John Milton | /023 |
| Chapter 4 | William Blake | /035 |
| Chapter 5 | William Wordsworth | /042 |
| Chapter 6 | Percy Bysshe Shelley | /053 |
| Chapter 7 | John Keats | /061 |
| Chapter 8 | Alfred Lord Tennyson | /071 |
| Chapter 9 | Robert Browning | /078 |
| Chapter 10 | William Butler Yeats | /086 |

**Part II　American Poets**

| | | |
|---|---|---|
| Chapter 11 | Emily Dickinson | /095 |
| Chapter 12 | Edgar Allan Poe | /103 |
| Chapter 13 | Ezra Pound | /109 |
| Chapter 14 | Henry Wadsworth Longfellow | /119 |

Chapter 15　Walt Whitman　　　　　　　　　　　　　　　　　　/126

Chapter 16　Robert Frost　　　　　　　　　　　　　　　　　　　/133

Chapter 17　T. S. Eliot　　　　　　　　　　　　　　　　　　　　/142

Chapter 18　Langston Hughes　　　　　　　　　　　　　　　　　/153

Chapter 19　William Carlos Williams　　　　　　　　　　　　　　/161

Chapter 20　Sylvia Plath　　　　　　　　　　　　　　　　　　　/169

Chapter 21　Allen Ginsberg　　　　　　　　　　　　　　　　　　/178

# Part I  English Poets

# Chapter 1

# Geoffrey Chaucer

Geoffrey Chaucer, the founder of English Poetry, was the son of a prosperous wine merchant. His creative works vividly reflected the changes which had taken root in English culture of the second half of the 14th century, which can be divided into three periods: the French period, the Italian period and the English period. In contradistinction to the old English alliterative verse, Chaucer chose the metrical form which laid the foundation of the rhymed stanzas of various types to English poetry. He also contributed to the foundation of the English literary language, the basis of which was formed by the London dialect, so profusely used by the poet.

## Critical Perspectives

### 1. Thematic Study

Ellen M. Caldwell, in "Love's (and Law's) Illusions in Chaucer's *Franklin's Tale*", not only examines the illusion of the marriage but also connects it to the equally illusory claim that Dorigen's hasty promise to Aurelius carries as much weight as her marriage vow or of any consciously worded statement where word and intent match. Finally, the mercy shown to Dorigen is assessed, not as the generous solution to Dorigen's waywardness but as an illusion that, like the law, pardons, but never exonerates, Dorigen and her unintended words.[①]

### 2. Reader-Oriented Criticism

C. W. R. D Moseley, in "*Tu Numeris Elementa Ligas*: The Consolation of Nature's Numbers in *Parlement of Foulys*", argues that Chaucer is expecting, indeed exploiting, the gap between the reception of a poem when it is heard socially and its afterlife as a text, when it is a different thing altogether. He also argues that a poem's form is itself a way of communicating ideas. The discussion focuses on *The Parlement of Foulys*, but the conclusions may be more widely

---

① Caldwell E M. "Love's (and Law's) Illusions in Chaucer's *Franklin's Tale*". Studies in Philology, 2019, 116:209-226.

applicable.①

Sebastian Sobecki, in "'And gret wel Chaucer whan ye mete': Chaucer's Earliest Readers, Addressees and Audiences", takes stock of what we know about Chaucer's earliest audiences, that is, about uses of and references to his work made during his lifetime. Relevant new research on manuscript use and ownership has been included in the case of Thomas Hoccleve and the scrivener Thomas Spencer. In addition to various named addressees of Chaucer's works—Peter Bukton, Henry Scogan and Philip de la Vache—this brief survey lists contemporary references to Chaucer and his works in the poetry of John Gower, Eustache Deschamps, John Clanvowe and Thomas Usk.②

## 3. Ethical Criticism

Chad G. Crosson, in "Chaucer's Corrective Form: *The Tale of Melibee* and the Poetics of Emendation", argues that the form Geoffrey Chaucer devises for *The Canterbury Tales* rests on a recursive and iterative corrective process based on grammatical emendation that was tied, by a long-standing analogy, to moral reform. *The Tale of Melibee* makes this process most explicit and suggests both the ambitions and the dangers of this artistic and moral project. On one hand, it is in the "Melibee" that the logic of the corrective process can be seen most clearly, as Prudence makes correction a principle of her prose; the tale portrays a slow, incremental repetition that only gradually brings about change. In that way, the tale displays the ambitions of the project. On the other hand, its dangers are clear

---

① Moseley C W R D. "*Tu Numeris Elementa Ligas*: The Consolation of Nature's Numbers in *Parlement of Foulys*". Critical Survey, 2017, 29(3):86-113.

② Sobecki S. "'And gret wel Chaucer whan ye mete': Chaucer's Earliest Readers, Addressees and Audiences". Critical Survey, 2017, 29(3):7-14.

enough, because the tale is notoriously unsatisfactory. Chaucer, however, deliberately stages those dangers in the "Melibee" and contrasts the dangers with a solution. While in the "Melibee" that incremental repetition illustrates literary pitfalls, in the "Tales" it becomes a means for literary innovation: the certainty of error and the corruption of discourse provide Chaucer an artistic method, one that evades moral clarity but provides the occasion for ongoing intellectual, artistic, and moral exercise. This account of Chaucer's moral poetics suggests that debates over the moral bearing of his poetry are unavoidable by design, but also irresolvable by design.①

## 4. New Criticism

Norm Klassen, in "The Coherence of Creation in the Word: The Rhetoric of Lines 1-34 of Chaucer's *General Prologue*", argues that Geoffrey Chaucer's introduction of the pilgrimage motif in lines 1-34 of the *General Prologue* to *The Canterbury Tales* combines the pursuit of the beatific vision with an evident interest in life in this world. Participation in God as coherence in Christ, who addresses and sustains the created order, informs the rhetorical structure and intensifying themes and playfulness of these lines. Resonant with the first sentence, the second performatively displays an obediential quality and emergent self and speciality, as Chaucer responds to the demands that the Incarnation places on the Christian poet.②

---

① Crosson C G. "Chaucer's Corrective Form: *The Tale of Melibee* and the Poetics of Emendation". Studies in Philogogy, 2018, 115(2):242-266.

② Klassen N. "The Coherence of Creation in the Word: The Rhetoric of Lines 1-34 of Chaucer's *General Prologue*". Christianity & Literature, 2014, 64(1):3-20.

Barry Windeatt, in "Chaucer's Tears", interprets of the many instances of weeping by Chaucer's characters, which is a key aspect of understanding his works. This article explores the relevance of models provided by tears in devotional contexts for viewing tears not simply as a corporeal symptom of emotion but as a mode of discourse that is as potent as it is paradoxical: both outward and inward, involuntary and applied, and forming a distinctive voice between passive and active.①

Helen Cooper, in "Unhap, Misadventure, Infortune: Chaucer's Vocabulary of Mischance", states that Chaucer is especially concerned with the use of privatives, negative prefixes, for these words, and the different senses they carry. In both positive and negative form, he recurrently works to inflect his larger concerns with Fortune (usually personified as an agent) and the mutability of the world.②

## 5. Archetypal Criticism

Benjamin Miele, in "The Political Unconscious of the Allusion: Shakespeare's Habits of Mind and the Cultural Politics of Reading Chaucer in Early Modern England", discusses about William Shakespeare's habits of mind and the cultural politics of reading poet Geoffrey Chaucer in early modern England. Topics discussed include allusion of contemporary ideologies; allusion created in the play *King Lear* by Shakespeare; and an account of a poem *The House of Fame* by Geoffrey Chaucer.③

---

① Windeatt B. "Chaucer's Tears". Critical Survey, 2018, 30(2): 74-93.
② Cooper H. "Unhap, Misadventure, Infortune: Chaucer's Vocabulary of Mischance". Critical Survey, 2017, 29(3): 15-26.
③ Miele B. "The Political Unconscious of the Allusion: Shakespeare's Habits of Mind and the Cultural Politics of Reading Chaucer in Early Modern England". Shakespeare Studies, 2017, 45: 144-150.

## 6. Narratology Study

R. S. Farris, in "Finding a Medievalist Narratology in Chaucer: Reinvention in *The Wife of Bath's Tale*", discusses medievalist narratology in the book, character of Beowulf in it, synchronization in narration, Romantic medievalism in literature and focus on audience familiarity. An overview of the book is also given.①

## 7. Cultural Study

Robert Epstein, in "The Lack of Interest in *The Shipman's Tale*: Chaucer and the Social Theory of the Gift", explores Bourdieu's theory of the gift in which all exchanges are fundamentally agonistic and motivated by individual profit and the criticism of economic anthropologist David Graeber's against such theory. It also examines Bourdieu's emphasis that conscious motivation is irrelevant.②

---

① Farris R S. "Finding a Medievalist Narratology in Chaucer: Reinvention in *The Wife of Bath's Tale*". Essays in Medieval Studies, 2016,32:57-63.

② Epstein R. "The Lack of Interest in *The Shipman's Tale*: Chaucer and the Social Theory of the Gift". Modern Philology, 2015,113(1):27-48.

# Chapter 2
# William Shakespeare

Although Shakespeare devoted his genius primarily to the stage, he was the foremost lyric poet of his age. His authentic non-dramatic poetry consists of two long narrative poems and his sequence of 154 sonnets. They are rich in images, conceit, metaphors and symbols. He excels both in writing lyrical verse and poetry of great passion and agony. His style varies with different moods he expresses. It can be lyrical, poetical, ecstatic, pathetic, cynical, sarcastic, and ironic. Apart from his sonnets and long poems, his dramas are also poetry.

## Critical Perspectives

### 1. New Criticism

Lina Perkins Wilder, in "Reserved Character: Shorthand and the Immortality Topos in Shakespeare's Sonnets", argues that Shakespeare's sonnets lay claim to a quality of liveliness as both an effect of reading and an intrinsic feature of the verse that parallels the physical life of the human body; the term "character" provides one way to conceptualize both the sonnets' internal aspirations to immortality and the ways in which successive generations of readers participate in perpetuating their and their addressee's life, allowing the poems to create a temporal and physical present for themselves. The sonnets' treatment of the term "character"—and particularly their implicit allusions to the fashionable new skill of shorthand transcription of "taking by charactery"—highlights the practical and ethical challenges of locating poetic immortality between the engagement of readers and the liveness of verse. As recording technology and as a method of writing that combines idiosyncrasy and, paradoxically, both secrecy and openness, shorthand provides a theoretical model for reading Shakespeare's sonnets. Understanding Shakespeare's use of the term character has broad implications not only for our understanding of the immortality topos but also for theories of reading and writing.[1]

---

[1] Wilder L P. "Reserved Character: Shorthand and the Immortality Topos in Shakespeare's Sonnets". Studies in Philology, 2019, 116(3):478-505.

## 2. Structuralism

Liliya R. Sakaeva and Liya A. Kornilova, in "Structural Analysis of the Oxymoron in the Sonnets of William Shakespeare", studies the structural groups of oxymoron in the Russian and English languages. It is also relevant to study oppositional lexical units represented in heterogeneous system languages from the standpoint of linguistic and extra linguistic meanings, since the figures of contrast are inconceivable without the associative-emotional and evaluative qualifications of the objects of opposition. They give the analysis of the oxymoron's nature and its functions in two different-structured languages. The article has carried out lexical and semantic characteristics of oxymoron. In the linguistic literature there is no generalized, concrete and universal structural and semantic classification of this stylistic device. This study attempts to create a structural and semantic classification, combining all the existing varieties of this figure of contrast. The analysis is applied in the linguistic examination of the sonnets written by William Shakespeare. When studying, systemizing and analyzing the opposite units, it is extremely important to study their structural features. The main objective of this study is to identify and describe the types of oxymoron in the language of Shakespeare's sonnets. [1]

Reuven Tsur, in "Delivery Style and Listener Response in the Rhythmical Performance of Shakespeare's Sonnets", inquires into the aesthetic event of the rhythmical performance of poetry. This event typically contains a reciter, a poetic text, and a listener (though the reciter himself may be the listener, too). Poetic rhythm is accessible only through some kind of performance, vocalized or silent. Rhythmical performance is not a unitary phenomenon; one must distinguish between

---

[1] Sakaeva L R, Kornilova L A. "Structural Analysis of the Oxymoron in the Sonnets of William Shakespeare". Journal of History, Culture and Art Research, 2017, Special Issue, 6(5):409-414.

various delivery styles. The article aspires to give a fairly comprehensive description of the aesthetic event under the discussion. A pilot experiment suggests that apparently incompatible responses to the same delivery instance may result from the listeners' realization of different subsets of aspects of the same event. They may, therefore, be meaningfully discussed and compared. Reuven's assumption is that rhythmical performance and delivery style are determined by the poem's metric structure, the performer's aesthetic conceptions and vocal resources, and the constraints of the cognitive system. He concentrates on small-scale computer-aided analyses and comparisons of performances by leading British actors. Consequently, he focuses on recordings of only one line, the last line of Sonnet 129, from commercially—available recordings. [1]

## 3. Cultural Studies

Manfred Pfister, in "'Love Merchandized': Money in Shakespeare's Sonnets" argues that although analysing Shakespeare's sonnets in the context of "Shakespeare and Money" is not an obvious choice, he believes that Karl Marx's "The Power of Money" in his *Economic and Philosophic Manuscripts* are as relevant to the sonnets as they are to plays such as *Timon of Athens*. Manfred's reading of them foregrounds their dialogue with terms and developments in early modern banking and focus on metaphors of economic transaction that run through the whole cycle; indeed, a third of them figure love, its wealth and truth, use and abuse, in terms of investment in order to project an alternative economy beyond the self-alienating world of banking/financial gain. This imbrication of the erotic with the

---

[1] Tsur R. "Delivery Style and Listener Response in the Rhythmical Performance of Shakespeare's Sonnets". College Literature, 2006, 33(1):170-196.

economic comprises also the writing of love sonnets, a competitive game-like economic transaction. Soneteering is a way of "merchandizing love" that inevitably casts a capitalist shadow across the supposedly most sincere expression of love. ①

## 4. Reader-Oriented Criticism

Matthew Zarnowiecki, in "Responses to Responses to Shakespeare's Sonnets: More Sonnets", argues that Shakespeare's sonnets have been subject to myriad creative and critical responses from the first instances of their partial publication in 1599 (two sonnets in *The Passionate Pilgrim*), in 1609 (the first edition of *Shakespeare's Sonnets*, which included *A Lover's Complaint*), and in 1640 (the first edition of John Benson's *Poems. Written by Wil. Shakespeare. Gent.*). Throughout the nineteenth and early twentieth centuries, editors and commentators felt comfortable manipulating the order of sonnets as printed in the 1609 Quarto, often in order to arrive at a presumed authorial intention, or to demonstrate more clearly the ways in which the sonnets tell the story of Shakespeare's life and times. The late twentieth and early twenty-first centuries have seen a different, but related phenomenon: a set of creative reimaginings, adaptations, and appropriations that attempt not only to bring Shakespeare's sonnets into new contexts, but also to respond to the sonnets while still remaining in their purview. This article explores these responses, especially instances in which poets, directors, dramatists, and film-makers seem to want to create something of their own but still remain faithful to Shakespeare in one way or another. Matthew's interest is in exploring that dual

---

① Pfister M. "'Love Merchandized': Money in Shakespeare's Sonnets". Critical Survey, 2018, 30(3):57-66.

desire, and it seems only fair, after exploring several versions of it, to offer one of his own.①

## 5. Canonization Study

Alan Forrest Hickman, in "'Subject to Invent': Adaptations of Shakespeare's Sonnets into other Media" argues that adaptation of Shakespeare's plays has been part of his legacy from the beginning, as works by artists such as Nahum Tate, Henry Purcell, and John Dryden can attest. Shakespeare's sonnets, too, have been put to many uses over the years. They have been set to music, they have been quoted by politicians, they have been used as wedding vows, and they have appeared on greeting cards. For many, they represent the ultimate statement on love. In the four hundred years since Shakespeare's death, they have found their way into a variety of media, including music, drama, books, television, and film. Whereas the plays have long been acknowledged as a rich source of inspiration—both serious and parodic—by artists and auteurs, ranging in kind from novelist James Joyce to dramatist Tom Stoppard to comedian Ben Elton, the poems have received less scrutiny in this regard. However, they represent a gold mine of untold riches, especially in terms of biography, which has yet to be sufficiently tapped. In this paper Alan takes a look at the various uses the sonnets have been put to, primarily in books, television, and film, and come to some conclusions regarding their success in remediation.②

Carl D. Atkins, in "The Importance of Compositorial Error and Variation to

---

① Zarnowiecki M. "Responses to Responses to Shakespeare's Sonnets: More Sonnets". Critical Survey, 2016, 28(2):10-26.

② Hickman A F. "'Subject to Invent': Adaptations of Shakespeare's Sonnets into other Media". Linguaculture, 2017(1):83-93.

the Emendation of Shakespeare's Texts: A Bibliographic Analysis of Benson's 1640 Text of *Shakespeare's Sonnets*", discusses the 1640 edition of poet William Shakespeare's "Sonnets" edited by John Benson and the significance of the editorial decisions Benson made in relation to previous publications. Carl contends that analysis of the Benson text is important because several later editions of "Sonnets" were based upon his work, and because we can compare them to previous publications of *Shakespeare's Sonnets* in various sources. ①

Carl D. Atkins, in "The Application of Bibliographical Principles to the Editing of Punctuation in *Shakespeare's Sonnets*", discusses the application of biographical principles to the editing of punctuation in dramatist William Shakespeare's sonnets; absence of English spelling standardization in the 16th century; repunctuation of the sonnet according to the understanding of the editors; implication of the absence of no system to Shakespearean punctuation. ②

## 6. New Historicism

David A. Harper, in "Revising Obsession in Shakespeare's Sonnets 153 and 154" reevaluates Shakespeare's sonnets 153 and 154 within the context of the 1609 Quarto, suggesting that only one of these anacreontics properly belongs to the sequence. The article first considers other moments of unintentional repetition in Shakespeare's corpus to provide evidence that Shakespeare's manuscript cancellations may have been overlooked by printers. Using the bibliographic features of the Quarto; Sonnet 153's thematic and formal linkages to the preceding

---

① Atkins C D. "The Importance of Compositorial Error and Variation to the Emendation of Shakespeare's Texts: A Bibliographic Analysis of Benson's 1640 Text of *Shakespeare's Sonnets*". Studies in Philology, 2007, 104(3):306-339.

② Atkins C D. "The Application of Bibliographical Principles to the Editing of Punctuation in *Shakespeare's Sonnets*". Studies in Philology, 2003, 100(4):493-513.

sequence, and the aptness of 153 rather than 154 as a bridge to *A Lover's Complaint*, the article argues that Shakespeare's likely cancellation of 154 was ignored in Eld's print shop for convenience or aesthetic concerns. While we may never know what shape *Shakespeare's Sonnets* took in manuscript, this article reclaims 153 as an important conclusion to the sequence, challenging a tradition of criticism in which the curious doubling of these two sonnets has often removed them from serious consideration.①

Reiko Oya, in "'Talk to Him': Wilde, his Friends, and Shakespeare's 'Sonnets'", discusses the interrelationships between Oscar Wilde, his lover Alfred Douglas, his editor Frank Harris, and George Bernard Shaw. It notes the drama created in all of their lives by Wilde's trial for obscenity in his novel *The Picture of Dorian Gray*. It discusses the role of the sonnets of William Shakespeare in helping them all probe the depths of their feelings towards Wilde, as evidenced in letters they wrote to each other and to others.②

MacDonald P. Jackson, in "Shakespeare's Sonnet CXI and John Davies of Hereford's *Microcosmos* (1603)", argues that lines in Shakespeare's Sonnet CXI bear a strong resemblance to lines in John Davies of Hereford's *Microcosmos* (1603). In the sonnet Shakespeare's Poet persona blames Fortune for making him reliant on "public means which public manners breeds". It has been widely supposed that Shakespeare is alluding to his career as player and playwright. Davies pays a backhanded compliment to Shakespeare as a poet of noble accomplishments, even though the stage "doth taint pure gentle blood". Davies's remarks, with their reminder of the social stigma attached to acting, were probably the stimulus for Shakespeare's sonnet, rather than a response to it, as editors have suggested.

---

① Harper D A. "Revising Obsession in Shakespeare's Sonnets 153 and 154". Studies in Philology, 2015, 112(1): 114-138.

② Oya R. "'Talk to Him': Wilde, his Friends, and Shakespeare's 'Sonnets'". Critical Survey, 2009, 21(3): 22-40.

Contexts for both poems are examined, including Davies's further comments on actors. ①

## 7. Translation Study

Olivia Landry, in "Verbal Performance in Dorothea Tieck's Translation of Shakespeare's Sonnets", studies the translation of William Shakespeare's sonnets by Dorothea Tieck. It says that the theory of double voicing by Mikhail Bakhtin is adopted to create an impetus for thinking about Tieck's sonnet translations as moments of verbal performance that engage the Shakespearean texts in a dialogue. It adds that the translation by Tieck yields an affirmation of her creative authorship as an essential translator. ②

Sara Guyer, in "Breath, Today: Celan's Translation of Shakespeare's Sonnet 71", analyzes the translation of William Shakespeare's sonnet 71 into German language by Paul Celan. The invitation given to Celan to translate the sonnets returned him to a style of poetry that seemed to him no longer a legitimate means of expression in the present. His translation of sonnet 71 reflects the extent to which translation can translate poetry and its tropes. In this translation, he remembers and repeats the sonnet's command: Forget the dead. Sonnet 71 is a poem that works by way of a series of turns and reversals implemented in the movement of each line. ③

---

① Jackson M D P. "Shakespeare's Sonnet CXI and John Davies of Hereford's *Microcosmos* (1603)". The Modern Language Review, 2007, 102(1):1-10.
② Landry O. "Verbal Performance in Dorothea Tieck's Translation of Shakespeare's Sonnets". Women in German Yearbook, 2012, 28:1-22.
③ Guyer S. "Breath, Today: Celan's Translation of Shakespeare's Sonnet 71". Comparative Literature, 2005, 57(4):328-351.

## 8. Reader-Oriented Criticism

Mario Aquilina, in "'Let me (not) read you': Countersigning Shakespeare's Sonnet 116", carries out a reading of Shakespeare's Sonnet 116 ("Let me not to the marriage of true minds") by following the complex movement of the "pas" (step/stop) that both invites and limits interpretation. Not only does Shakespeare's sonnet demand such a reading, thus prospectively and retroactively entering a dialogue with Blanchot and Derrida's writing, but the sonnet also enacts the iterable logic of the signature and countersignature by reading itself in terms of the (im)possibility of reading. Exploring the possibility of defining love through various forms of negation and slippery metaphors, Sonnet 116 is always already implicated in a discourse on singularity and the general law, the proper and the common, the mark and the re-mark that invites further countersignatures despite the impression that the numerous commentaries on the sonnet through the ages might have exhausted the poem's openness to new readings.[①]

## 9. Narratology Study

Stephen X. Mead, in "Shakespeare's Play with Perspective: Sonnet 24, *Hamlet*, *Lear*", argues that indebted to Shakespeare's understanding of perspective in the visual arts as much as to the tradition of ut pictura poesis, Sonnet 24 uses poetry's capacity for ambiguity and references drama's ability to create slippage between character and actor to demonstrate that manipulated surfaces—to wit, the

---

① Aquilina M. "'Let me (not) read you': Countersigning Shakespeare's Sonnet 116". Word and Text: A Journal of Literary Studies and Linguistics, 2011,1(2):79-90.

perspectival paintings in vogue since the early fifteenth century—cannot delve into the interior but only discover, or create, more surfaces. By understanding and to some degree exploiting the techniques of perspectival artists, Shakespeare is gradually able to create a play space at once deeply physical and insistently metaphysical. The chamber scene in *Hamlet*, with its mirror and thrust-through arras, and the final scene in *King Lear*, with its stage-versioned vanishing point at the silent mouth of the dead Cordelia, suggest that Shakespeare uses his knowledge of perspective and its limitations in part to explore the dramatic possibilities for character interiority. [1]

Danijela Kambaskovic-Sawyers, in "Three Themes in One, which Wondrows Scope Affords: Ambiguous Speaker and Storytelling in Shakespeare's Sonnets", presents a criticism on the ambiguous speaker and storytelling in the sonnet sequences of William Shakespeare in referencing to other works of some poets. It argues that ambiguous speakers appear and perform their integrating functions in Petrarch's sonnet sequences as well as all the major sonnet sequences of the Elizabethan period. However, the difference between Shakespeare's and other great Elizabethan sonnet sequences lies in the degree and complexity of his main character's ambiguity, as well as in the skill with which this complexity is managed. [2]

## 10. Feminist Criticism

Regula Hohl Trillini, in " The Gaze of the Listener: Shakespeare's Sonnet

---

[1] Mead S X. "Shakespeare's Play with Perspective: Sonnet 24, *Hamlet*, *Lear*". Studies in Philology, 2012, 109(3):225-257.

[2] Kambaskovic-Sawyers D. "Three Themes in One, which Wondrows Scope Affords: Ambiguous Speaker and Storytelling in Shakespeare's Sonnets". Criticism, 2007, 49(3):285-305.

128 and Early Modern Discourses of Music and Gender", argues that from the Tudor period on, keyboard skills were a staple in the education of girls of "quality". However, theoretical admiration of music and musical skill always co-existed with wariness of actual performers and performances. The hyperbolic musical metaphors for love and marriage contrast with a near-complete absence of harmony and edification in representations of actual music-making. Those two main literary uses of music represent the period's acutely ambivalent discourse on music as well as women, both of which may be perceived as divinely admirable or hellishly tempting. Literary references, to keyboard playing favour the latter: the virginals are regularly associated with lewdness and sexual availability. This general discursive and historical background, as well as the literary tropes associated with the virginals inform a new reading of Shakespeare's Sonnet 128, whose much-deprecated cruxes and mixed metaphors are read not as authorial oversights but as a significant elaboration of contradictions in the English course on musical performance, particularly when undertaken by women.[①]

M. L. Stapleton, in "Making the Woman of Him: Shakespeare's Man Right Fair as Sonnet Lady", presents the gender and sexuality content of the "Man Right Fair" sonnet by William Shakespeare; discussion on the homoeroticism content of the sonnet; analysis of each line of the sonnet; characteristics of the characters portrayed in the sonnet".[②]

## 11. Gender Study

Amanda Rudd, in "A Fair Youth in the Forest of Arden: Reading Gender and

---

[①] Trillini R H. "The Gaze of the Listener: Shakespeare's Sonnet 128 and Early Modern Discourses of Music and Gender". Music & Letters, 2008, 89(1):1-17.

[②] Stapleton M L. "Making the Woman of Him: Shakespeare's Man Right Fair as Sonnet Lady". Texas Studies in Literature and Language. 2004, 46(3):271-295.

Desire in *As You Like It* and Shakespeare's Sonnets", highlights a challenge to orthodox constructions of gender posed by the play. It explains the absence of homosexual characters in the play. The link between the development of ideal country love and the introduction of the fair youth to the Forest of Arden in England is also discussed. ①

Casey Charles, in "Was Shakespeare Gay? Sonnet 20 and the Politics of Pedagogy", discusses questions the sexual identity of William Shakespeare; how pedagogical method is implicated in the controversy over the interpretation of Shakespeare's Sonnet 20; role of a teacher in imparting knowledge to students; how can Sonnet 20 provide a clue to the nature of the poet's purpose. ②

## 12. Historiography

Dean Keith Simonton, in "Shakespeare's Sonnets: A Case of and for Single-Case Historiometry", argues that the two oldest forms of psychohistory, as generically defined, are psychobiography (idiographic, qualitative, and single-case) and historiometry (nomothetic, quantitative, and multiple-case). In practice this distinction gets blurred, both because psychobiography is often nomothetic (e g, psychoanalytic) and after outlining the assets of single-case historiometry, a specific case is given in an analysis of the 154 sonnets of William Shakespeare. These sonnets were first reliably differentiated on aesthetic success according to an archival popularity measure, and then this relative merit was predicted using content analytical measures suggested by research on artistic creativity. The superior sonnets

---

① Rudd A. "A Fair Youth in the Forest of Arden: Reading Gender and Desire in *As You Like It* and Shakespeare's Sonnets". The Wooden O Symposium, 2009, 9:106-117.
② Charles C. "Was Shakespeare Gay? Sonnet 20 and the Politics of Pedagogy". College Literature, 1998, 25(3):35.

treat specific themes, display considerable thematic richness in the number of issues discussed, exhibit greater linguistic complexity as gauged by such objective measures as the type-token ratio and adjective-verb quotient, and feature more primary process imagery (using Martindale's Regressive Imagery Dictionary). After discussing how these results can enlarge our general understanding of artistic creativity as well as our specific appreciation of Shakespeare's creativity, the potential application of single-case historiometry to intrinsically psychobiographical problems is examined.[①]

---

① Simonton D K. "Shakespeare's Sonnets: A Case of and for Single-Case Historiometry". Journal of Personality, 1989, 57(3):695-721.

# Chapter 3
# John Milton

Milton was born in Bread Street, Cheapside, and the elder son of a self-made businessman. In his life, Milton showed himself a real revolutionary, a master poet and a great prose writer. He fought for freedom in all aspects as a Christian humanist, while his achievements in literature made him tower over all the other English writers of his time and exerted a great influence over later ones. Milton's literary achievements can be divided into three groups: the early poetic works, the middle prose pamphlets and the last great poems. He is a master of the blank verse. He first used blank verse in non-dramatic works, which has frequently been called "Miltonic style". Here, his own genius for poetry and matchless daring in experiment introduced variety and achieved extraordinary freedom. In *Paradise Lost*, he acquires an absolute mastery of the blank verse. Another characteristic of his style is the use of allusions to other works, especially classic works.

## Critical Perspectives

### 1. Thematic Study

Paul Cefalu, in "Incarnational Apophatic: Rethinking Divine Accommodation in John Milton's *Paradise Lost*", argues that John Milton's *Paradise Lost* reveals both the limits and dangers of several modes of accommodating God to both angelic and human understanding. Not only does God fail successfully to accommodate himself and his internally efficient decrees during the celestial council, but the Son, who might otherwise serve as an agent of the special accommodation of redemption, also fails to accommodate the Father: the Son's tendency to disclose several of God's mysteries subverts the basic concealing-revealing function of accommodation, which otherwise aims to render some of God's ways palatable to creaturely understanding even while ensuring the ontological and epistemological distance between creatures and God. Milton thus approaches accommodation skeptically, even testing its effectiveness and capaciousness as an exegetical device that might be of use in mimetic poetry.[①]

### 2. Canonization Study

Gary Kuchar, in "Milton, Shakespeare, and Canadian Confederation: Thomas

---

① Cefalu P. "Incarnational Apophatic: Rethinking Divine Accommodation in John Milton's *Paradise Lost*". Studies in Philology, 2016, 113(1):198-228.

D'Arcy McGee as Literary Critic", argues that while John Milton's influence on the founding of the American republic is well documented, his presence in Canadian Confederation remains virtually unknown. Yet Milton is a significant figure in the work of Thomas D'Arcy McGee, the so-called "prophet of Canadian Confederation." Revealingly, McGee's interpretation of Milton as a moderate Christian humanist differs significantly from the more dominant American reception of him as a political and religious radical. Similarly, McGee's defence of constitutional monarchy finds support in his reading of Shakespeare as an ideal embodiment of the supposed Elizabethan synthesis of monarchical and republican traditions. Ultimately, McGee's conservative reading of Milton reinforced his mature political, constitutional, and social vision, whereas his reading of Shakespeare actively shaped it. ①

## 3. Marxist Criticism

Jude Welburn, in "Divided Labors: Work, Nature, and the Utopian Impulse in John Milton's *Paradise Lost*", argues that utopia has often been defined as an imaginary, this-worldly, rational ideal distinct from older, mythic, prepolitical forms of social ideality such as Paradise or the Golden Age. Milton's *Paradise Lost* complicates this opposition and departs from exegetical tradition, introducing temporality, materiality, and social organization into the Genesis story. The chaotic vitality of nature in Milton's paradise makes Adam and Eve's labor meaningful and necessary, and the preservation of the Edenic state is predicated upon the control of excess and a rational division of work and play. Milton's paradise is not, therefore,

---

① Kuchar G. "Milton, Shakespeare, and Canadian Confederation: Thomas D'Arcy McGee as Literary Critic". University of Toronto Quarterly, 2019, 88(1):1-23.

simply a state of nature, a presocial or prepolitical condition; it is the seed-form of a larger social order that already contains within itself the problem of the metabolism of nature and society. If paradise and utopia form an opposition, this opposition is internal to *Paradise Lost*.[①]

## 4. Archetypal Criticism

David V. Urban, in "John Milton, Paradox, and the Atonement: Heresy, Orthodoxy, and the Son's Whole-Life Obedience", demonstrates that Milton's orthodox presentation of the Crucifixion and the substitutionary atonement is predicated on his orthodox presentation of Jesus's whole-life obedience, a perfect obedience to God and his law that substitutes for the disobedience of those who put their faith in Jesus. This presentation, evident in *Paradise Lost*, *Upon the Circumcision*, *Paradise Regained*, and *De Doctrina Christiana*, is consistent with presentations in various orthodox sixteenth-and seventeenth-century reformed documents. Paradoxically, however, Milton's presentational emphasis on the orthodox notion of Jesus's whole-life obedience is likely predicated upon his heterodox views regarding the deity of the Son of God.[②]

## 5. New Historicism

Giuseppina Iacono Lobo, in "John Milton, Oliver Cromwell, and the Cause of Conscience", discusses Milton's sonnet of 1652 addressed to the then Lord General

---

① Welburn J. "Divided Labors: Work, Nature, and the Utopian Impulse in John Milton's *Paradise Lost*". Studies in Philology, 2019, 116(3):506-538.

② Urban D V. "John Milton, Paradox, and the Atonement: Heresy, Orthodoxy, and the Son's Whole-Life Obedience". Studies in Philology, 2015, 112(4):817-836.

Cromwell, this article provides a more complex understanding of the much-examined relationship between the poet-polemicist and eventual Lord Protector. More specifically, Giuseppina argues that their shared dedication to liberty of conscience makes Milton's covert or complete repudiation of Cromwell unlikely. While Cromwell's dismissal of an elected body and his assumption of power seem to conflict with Milton's championing of religious and civil liberty, if we consider more closely the language of and occasion for Milton's sonnet, it is clear that Milton dismissed the Rump Parliament long before Cromwell ever did. [1]

Curry Kennedy, in "Milton's Ethos, English Nationhood, and the Fast-Day Tradition in Areopagitica", argues that during the English Revolution, Westminster divines Cornelius Burges and Stephen Marshall resurrected the practice of preaching in Parliament in an attempt to articulate, without repair to kingship or Catholicism, what it meant to be free, godly, and English. Though scholars have acknowledged Areopagitica's debt to the nation-forming biblical rhetoric of these sermons, in this study curry argues that Milton commandeers that rhetoric—especially the application of the figure of Israel to the would-be commonwealth—in order to renovate his own public image, such that he and the nation cannot be thought apart. Milton projects an ethos that is at once representative and apostolic, Isocratean and Pauline. At the same time, he reworks the sermons' figural depictions of England's divine election, covenant, and religious conformity such that his nation could not exist without him. This imbrication of persona and patria reconciles contrasting theories about Milton's self-understanding and extends our understanding of Milton's nationalism in a time of revolution and religious upheaval. [2]

---

[1] Lobo G I. "John Milton, Oliver Cromwell, and the Cause of Conscience". Studies in Philology, 2015, 112(4):774-797.

[2] Kennedy C. "Milton's Ethos, English Nationhood, and the Fast-Day Tradition in Areopagitica". Studies in Philology, 2019, 116(2):375-400.

Christopher N. Warren, in "John Milton and the Epochs of International Law", argues that for the historian of international law William Grewe in his controversial opus, The Epochs of International Law, it was the English writer John Milton who offered the death blow to an entire epoch, one founded on the principle that discovery brought legal title in international law. Yet John Milton's *Paradise Lost* is rarely considered alongside the history of international law. In this article, Christopher contends that a robust history of international law in the 17th century would profit from engaging head on with literary texts like *Paradise Lost*. Milton's understanding of the law of nations provides legal scholars with a richer intellectual history of 17th-century international law than that typically on offer—one more sensitive to humanist methods, literary texts, and embodied questions of vulnerability. Approaching the intellectual history of the law of nations dialectically, Christopher suggests that a full reckoning of Milton's law of nations in *Paradise Lost* requires a careful balance of presentism and openness to alterity—presentism in the sense that we might appreciate how strongly Milton's law of nations resonates with debates about international law in our own time, and alterity in the sense that Milton's law of nations encompassed much that many of today's readers would hardly recognize as "international law". A full intellectual history of Milton's law of nations, then, may require us partly to estrange that term—to set aside a priori definitions of the "international" and resist easy transhistorical transpositions from Milton's late Renaissance world to our own—but it also requires a paradoxical domestication of the law of nations, a making familiar, a bringing into one's home.[①]

Nicole A. Jacobs, in "John Milton's Beehive, from Polemic to Epic", argues that while the bee simile in book 1 of *Paradise Lost* has garnered much critical

---

① Warren C N. "John Milton and the Epochs of International Law". European Journal of International Law, 2013, 24(2):557-581.

attention, the significant image of the hive in Milton's corpus remains largely overlooked. Deriving from an ancient literary tradition, the bee metaphor was enlisted in seventeenth-century England as a divine symbol of monarchical and ecclesiastical power structures. From his polemic to his epic, Milton, by contrast, consistently uses apian imagery to register harsh critiques of earthly monarchy, feminine influence, and Catholic superstition. Beginning with an unexamined bee passage in Eikonoklastes, this article traces Milton's revisionist reading of the apiological kingdom, which culminates in his representation of insect and related serpentine imagery in *Paradise Lost*. Nicole argues that the Miltonic hive serves as a symbol of a natural corruption of the divine hierarchy, an inevitable failure to replicate on earth or in hell the benevolent design of heaven. [1]

Alison A. Chapman, in "Milton and Legal Reform", argues that the second half of the seventeenth century was the first great period of legal reform in England's history. This article situates John Milton in relationship to this contemporary context, arguing that he comments frequently on the need to change England's laws and displays a finely tuned awareness of some of the major legal debates of his time. This article surveys Milton's writings about the law and legal education, and it concludes by examining his 1659-1660 political pamphlets where he calls for reform of the judicial system and the establishment of local courts. [2]

Christopher Crosbie, in "Publicizing the Science of God: Milton's Raphael and the Boundaries of Knowledge", discusses how poet John Milton handles his representations of science through a sustained inquiry into problematics of Raphael's narration and the social space through which he directs his pedagogical efforts. Topics discussed include an argument that Raphael's significance in

---

[1] Jacobs N A. "John Milton's Beehive, from Polemic to Epic". Studies in Philology, 2015, 112(4):798-816.

[2] Chapman A A. "Milton and Legal Reform". Renaissance Quarterly, 2016, 69(2):529-565.

*Paradise Lost* resides in his simultaneous representation of divergent, antithetical philosophies towards scientific knowledge in the public sphere and the execution of Raphael's mission.①

## 6. Cultural Study

William Walker, in "John Milton's Magisterial Reformation", argues that in the English prose he published over a period of two decades, John Milton frequently uses the term "reformation" to identify the age in which he was living and the causes for which he was fighting. In so doing, he reveals his support for the magisterial Reformation and his rejection of the radical Reformation. He expresses his desire not for religious diversity but for union with the Scottish and Continental Reformed Churches. He constructs a complex discourse that is self-serving, misleading in some ways, prophetic, and calculated to win a range of polemical contests. In supporting the magisterial Reformation, he also displays his support for theologians who participate in government, and magistrates who participate in determining religious belief and conduct. Milton thus repudiates many aspects of modernity and is, as he insists, a man who lived during, and promoted what he called, "times of reformation".②

John G. Peters, in "Father, King, and God: John Milton's Prose Response to Monarchy", presents the work of the writer John Milton. It explains that during the Renaissance era of England, Milton was a dissenter against the idea of kings being divinely appointed by God. The writing of John Stubbs and William Prynne is

---

① Crosbie C. "Publicizing the Science of God: Milton's Raphael and the Boundries of Knowledge". Renascence, 2015, 67(4):239-260.

② Walker W. "John Milton's Magisterial Reformation". Reformation & Renaissance Review, 2016, 18(2):174-194.

discussed and the social implications of Milton's ideology are examined. The relationship between family, monarchy, and divinity is also explored. ①

## 7. Feminist Criticism

Dan Vogel, in "Eve— The First Feminist: John Milton's Midrash on Genesis 3:6", discusses the Midrash of John Milton on the ambiguity of the word "with her" (imah) in Genesis 3:6, which he describes in Book ix of *Paradise Lost*. It says that Milton's Midrash, which was composed from clues he developed from Rabbi David Kimhi, states that Adam was called by Eve from other place from the garden to eat the fruit together with her. It explores Milton's hints for Eve as a feminist with Eve's proposal to Adam to divide their labor and her desire for independence. ②

Robert Crossley, in "Alone in the Center: Brynhild and Brünnhilde", argues that heroic narratives classical Western literature have few memorable women at their center and cites reference to poet John Milton's Eve presented like Son of the God. It mentions that sagas of medieval Iceland present a challenge to readers who bring to these narratives of family feuds the expectations either of southern European epic or of the modern psychological novel. ③

## 8. Canonization Study

Patrick Madigan, in "Game Over", offers insights on the influence of John

---

① Peters J G. "Father, King, and God: John Milton's Prose Response to Monarchy". Midwest Quarterly, 2008, 49(3):228-244.

② Vogel D. "Eve—the First Feminist: John Milton's Midrash on Genesis 3:6". Jewish Bible Quarterly, 2012, 40(1):19-24.

③ Crossley R. "Alone in the Center: Brynhild and Brünnhilde". The Massachusetts Review, 2018, 59(3):490-504.

Milton as a poet and author of the book *Paradise Lost* particularly on his character Lucifer or Satan. It mentions that the character that was in Satan was emulated in other literature from other countries including the "of Dante Alegheiri's Divine Comedy".[①]

Lisa Ampleman, in "The Original Antihero", offers literary criticism of the epic poem *Paradise Lost*, by John Milton, noting the role of Satan in the poem. Topics include comparisons of Milton's work to films, the notion of Satan as a sympathetic antihero, and the relation of Milton's blindness to the poem. The depiction of the marriage of the biblical figures Adam and Eve in the poem is noted.[②]

Adam Foley, in "Miltonic Sublimity and the Crisis of Wolffianism before Kant", discusses the importance of poet John Milton on the development of British Romanticism and the crisis of Wolffianism before German philosopher Immanuel Kant. Topics include the role of Milton in minimizing rationalism for the Swiss, the two principles that formed the foundation of his poetics namely the principles of non-contradiction and of sufficient reason, and Kant's complaint about the license of Wolff's speculative metaphysics to claim access to the monumenal world.[③]

## 9. New Criticism

Travis D. Williams, in "Unspeakable Creation: Writing in *Paradise Lost* and Early Modern Mathematics", offers poetry criticism of the poem *Paradise Lost* by John Milton. It focuses on the contrast between literal eyesight and the perception of a clearer sight of the mind. It mentions the rhetorical and poetic devices employed

---

① Madigan P. "Game Over". Heythrop Journal, 2018, 59(1):84-97.
② Ampleman L. "The Original Antihero". America, 2018, 219(9):18-20.
③ Foley A. "Miltonic Sublimity and the Crisis of Wolffianism before Kant". Journal of the History of Ideas, 2017, 78(1):51-71.

by poets in mimicry of the deity's accommodation. It outlines the efforts in the poem to facilitate access to the perfect and divine by limited noetic and aesthetic capacities to make a success of accommodation.①

David Macey, in "Who Is Pressing You Now?: A Reconsideration of Milton's *Pyrrha Ode*", discusses English poet John Milton's translation of Roman poet Horace's Odes or the *Pyrrha Ode*. Topics covered include the rendering's metaphrastic quality in its mirroring of Latin diction and syntax, the issues of translation date, relation to Milton's stylistic development, and poetic merits, and the view that Milton presents his version as a parallel text rather than as a substitute for the Horace original. Also noted are the Milton translation's ingenuity and shortcomings.②

## 10. Biographical Analysis

Morris Freedman, in "John Milton and the King of Poland", presents a biographical analysis of the work of John Milton. In 1674, the last year of his life, John Milton translated from the Latin what might be described today as a press release by a foreign power, Poland. It announced the election of John Sobieski as the country's new king. The document did not carry Milton's name. Why did Milton undertake what must have been, certainly at that late point in his career, such an unusual, not to say bizarre, task? He had completed and, in the preceding six years, had published the three great works which established his reputation: *Paradise Lost*, *Paradise Regained*, and *Samson Agonistes*. He was widely accepted as the great poet of his time. Personages in England and from the continent visited

---

① Williams T D. "Unspeakable Creation: Writing in *Paradise Lost* and Early Modern Mathematics". Philological Quarterly, 2019, 98(1 & 2): 181-200.

② Macey D. "Who Is Pressing You Now?: A Reconsideration of Milton's *Pyrrha Ode*". Philological Quarterly, 2016, 95(3/4): 425-448.

and honored him. Andrew Marvell, as a member of parliament under Charles II, had not only helped protect him against royalist retribution after the Restoration, but had added his encomium to an edition of *Paradise Lost*.[①]

## 11. Cognitive Study

Joshua R. Held, in "Eve's 'paradise within' in *Paradise Lost*: A Stoic Mind, a Love Sonnet, and a Good Conscience", argues that the "paradise within, happier farr" that the angel Michael foretells in the final book of Milton's *Paradise Lost* has attracted widespread and often divisive comment. The most significant interpretive context for the phrase directly follows Michael's speech. When Adam returns to the newly wakened Eve, she greets him with a blank verse love sonnet that triangulates three sources of encouragement for the couple in their coming exile from Eden. Each source unveils a different aspect of the "paradise within": the Stoic trope of the world as a homeland, the Renaissance love motif of the lover as a world, and the divine peace of conscience, which many contemporaries described as a "paradise within".[②]

---

[①] Freedman M. "John Milton and the King of Poland". Virginia Quarterly Review, 1991, 67(4): 687-688.

[②] Held J R. "Eve's 'paradise within' in *Paradise Lost*: A Stoic Mind, a Love Sonnet, and a Good Conscience". Studies in Philology, 2017, 114(1):171-196.

# Chapter 4
# William Blake

Of all the romantic poets of the eighteenth century, Blake is the most distinctive one. Blake's first book of poems, *Poetical Sketches*, which he had printed when he was twenty-six years old, showed his dissatisfaction with the reigning poetic tradition and his restless quest for new form and techniques. Blake can be claimed to be the first important Romantic poet, showing contempt for the rule of reason, opposing the classical tradition of the eighteenth century, and treasuring the individual's imagination. Blake wrote his poems in plain and direct language. His poems often carry the lyric beauty with profound meaning. He distrusted the abstract and tends to embody his views with visual images. Symbolism to some extent is an evident feature of his poetry.

## Critical Perspectives

### 1. Feminist Criticism

Lucy Cogan, in "William Blake's *The Book of Los* and the Female Prophetic Tradition", talks about author William Blake's book *The Book of Los* and his documented encounter with a female prophet. It discusses Blake's attitude towards women and religion. Blake's works also include millenarianism of his times and the role of gender in prophetic speech. Blake's deception of imaginative redemption in discussed.[①]

### 2. Eco-Criticism

M. A. Elma Dedovic-Atilla and Senad Becirovic, in "Human Image in Blake's Poetry", explores the representation of the human in William Blake's poetry. In order to grasp depiction of humankind in all its depth, a number of constructs in close relation to the human image are being investigated including the role and nature of God, nature, animal world, as well as the place and illustration of the world of children and adults. All of the concepts are examined in regards to the poet's dichotomist depiction of the concepts in his both earlier and later literary works, culminating in the ultimate reconciliation and reunion of the seemingly

---

① Cogan L. "William Blake's *The Book of Los* and the Female Prophetic Tradition". Romanticism, 2015, 21(1):48-58.

opposing perceptions within the later literary writings. ①

## 3. Canonization Study

Thora Brylowe, in "Of Gothic Architects and Grecian Rods: William Blake, Antiquarianism and the History of Art", focuses on the anticlassicism of British artist William Blake and how it impacted his interpretation of art history. Thora explains the relationship between classical antiquarians and British connoisseurship, explores why Blake's feelings towards antiquarianism and Hellenism changed throughout his life, and examines how Irish scientist William Hamilton influenced Blake's work. ②

## 4. New Historicism

Angus Whitehead, in "'Humble but Respectable': Recovering the Neighbourhood Surrounding William and Catherine Blake's Last Residence, No. 3 Fountain Court, Strand, c. 1820-1827", draws upon a wide range of unpublished archival sources, Angus presents a detailed reconstruction of Fountain Court and its residents, William and Catherine Blake during the period William and Catherine Blake were resident at No. 3 Fountain Court (c. 1820-1827). The paper presents important new information concerning the society and milieu in Fountain Court and its neighbourhood during 1820-1827. This fresh archival evidence enables us to identify and precisely locate for the first time the "humble but respectable" fellow

---

① Dedovic-Atilla M A E, Becirovic S. "Human Image in Blake's Poetry". European Researcher, 2018, 9(4):284-290.
② Brylowe T. "Of Gothic Architects and Grecian Rods: William Blake, Antiquarianism and the History of Art". Romanticism, 2012, 18(1):89-104.

lodgers and neighbours living in Fountain Court during William and Catherine Blake's period of residence, and provides a detailed picture of life in the Blakes' neighbourhood during this period, and of trades conducted in the court, as well as the close familial and social relationships existing between a number of households immediately surrounding the Blakes' residence. Such relationships provide a context for William and Catherine's own relationships with their brother-in-law and landlord at 3 Fountain Court, Henry Banes and his wife Sarah Banes (née Boucher) and two of their neighbours and fellow lodgers in the court, the carver and gilder John George Lohr, and Blake's employer and fellow artist John Barrow. The Blakes' last residence was not in a sleepy, forgotten backwater, as some contemporary accounts and later biographers appear to suggest. As my paper demonstrates, Fountain Court in the 1820s, leading directly off the Strand, a major commercial thoroughfare of the largest metropolis of the period, was comprised of a small community, thriving with social and commercial activity. The reconstruction provides a detailed immediate context in which to view afresh William and Catherine's years living and working in Fountain Court.[1]

Morton D. Paley, in "William Blake's *Milton/A Poem* and the Miltonic Matrix of 1791-1810", argues that from the time when "Milton lovd me in childhood & shewd me his face", William Blake felt a special relationship with John Milton. He would therefore have felt a great interest in the extraordinary spate of publishing and pictorial activity (sometimes both together) that occurred in the last decade of the eighteenth century and the early years of the nineteenth. He was, indeed, mentioned as a participant in two major Milton projects planned during this period, but neither materialized. His own *Milton/A Poem*, completed c. 1811, addresses

---

[1] Whitehead A. "'Humble but Respectable': Recovering the Neighbourhood Surrounding William and Catherine Blake's Last Residence, No. 3 Fountain Court, Strand, c. 1820-1827". University of Toronto Quarterly, 2011, 80(4):858-879.

two major subjects of previous discussion: Milton's political commitment and his relations with the women in his life. Characteristically, Blake does not adopt any prior positions, but renders his own views, which are different from any of them. ①

Roland Boer, in "E. P. Thompson, Antinomianism, and the Theology of William Blake", presents a close engagement with the historian E. P. Thompson's reading of the artist and writer William Blake (1757-1827) in Witness Against the Beast (1993). In particular, the interest is in the way Thompson comes to a theological insight through his interaction with Blake (this article is therefore not a study of Blake himself). Thompson explores Blake's writings and art, his connections with radical Dissenting groups in London, the light that the archives of the Muggletonians shed on such groups, and the theological positions of these groups. This search leads Thompson to identify the radical possibilities of Paul's doctrine of justification by faith. In the hands of these groups, the doctrine became a radical antinomian position with both theological and political ramifications. Thompson's insight is not merely to have (re-) discovered these radical possibilities, but also to have come to the position that religion and politics are inescapably interwoven. ②

Thomas J. J. Altizer, in "The Revolutionary Vision of William Blake", argues that it was William Blake's insight that the Christian churches, by inverting the Incarnation and the dialectical vision of Paul, have repressed the body, divided God from creation, substituted judgment for grace, and repudiated imagination, compassion, and the original apocalyptic faith of early Christianity. Blake's prophetic poetry thus contributes to the renewal of Christian ethics by a process of subversion and negation of Christian moral, ecclesiastical, and theological

---

① Paley M D. "William Blake's *Milton/A Poem* and the Miltonic Matrix of 1791-1810". University of Toronto Quarterly, 2011, 80(4):786-814.

② Boer R. "E. P. Thompson, Antinomianism, and the Theology of William Blake". Sino-Christian Studies, 2009, 8:31-52.

traditions, which are recognized precisely as inversions of Jesus, and therefore as instances of the forms of evil that God-in-Christ overcomes through Incarnation, reversing the Fall. Blake's great epic poems, particularly Milton (1804-1808) and Jerusalem (1804-1820), embody his heterodox representation of the final coincidence of Christ and Satan through which, at last, all things are made new.①

## 5. Comparative Study

Ryan J. Davidson, in "A Proposal for Revaluation: Points of Contact and Sides of Likeness between William Blake and Walt Whitman", proposes an approach to evaluate the relationship between William Blake and Walt Whitman. Ryan begins by grounding my proposal in a critical framework. It is framed by a book history approach, but also an approach to 19th century American literature as a post-colonial literature. In regards to the book history element he traces an outline of Blake's publication history and the poems of Blake's that Whitman might have encountered, then provides examples of the similarities between Blake and Whitman. This paper concludes with a discussion of the implications it may have on ideas of literary influence. This is the beginning of a much larger project wherein Ryan traces the actual influences which created the similarities that he outlines here".②

## 6. Reader-oriented Criticism

Andreea Paris-Popa, in "William Blake's *The Tyger* as an Expression of the

---

① Altizer T J J. "The Revolutionary Vision of William Blake". Journal of Religious Ethics, 2009, 37(1):33-38.
② Davidson R J. "A Proposal for Revaluation: Points of Contact and Sides of Likeness between William Blake and Walt Whitman". Hawliyat, 2018(18):61-76.

Reader's Futile Search for Authorial Intent", discusses that reader response criticism warns against the literary interpreter's endeavor to uncover the author's intention in order to reconstruct the original meaning of the literary text. The present essay aims at providing a way of understanding this fundamental critical fallacy from the perspective of reader response criticism by allowing for this critical stance to be emphasized with the help of literature, and more specifically, of William Blake's famous *Songs of Innocence and of Experience* poem *The Tyger*. In this perspective, the poem can be seen as stressing the potential futile quest for authorial intent in the process of literary interpretation, as well as the consequences of perceiving the literary text as an echo of its creator rather than a reader-reflected image and the interpretative perils associated with an insistent quest on the part of the reader to discover the origin of the text to the detriment of a creative construction of meaning. [1]

---

[1] Paris-Popa A. "William Blake's *The Tyger* as an Expression of the Reader's Futile Search for Authorial Intent". East-West Cultural Passage, 2016, 16(1):110-119.

# Chapter 5

# William Wordsworth

William Wordsworth was born in Cockermouth in West Cumberland, just on the northern fringe of the English Lake District. When Wordsworth's mother died, the eight-year-old boy was sent to school at Hawkshead, near Esthwaite Lake, in the heart of that thinly settled region whereafter he and Coleridge transformed into the poetic center of England. Wordsworth is above all the poet of the remembrance of things past, or as he himself put it, of "emotion recollected in tranquility." Some objects or events in the present triggers a sudden renewal of feelings he had experienced in youth; the result is a poem exhibiting the sharp discrepancy between what Wordsworth called "two consciousnesses": himself as he is now and himself as he once was. Wordsworth is at his best in his poetry of nature. As a great poet of nature, he found that nature means more than rivers, trees, rocks, mountains, lakes, and so on. Nature has a moral value and has its philosophical significance. In his poems, Wordsworth aimed at simplicity and purity of language, fighting against the conventional forms of the 18th century poetry.

## Critical Perspectives

### 1. Philosophical Study

William A. Ulmer, in "William Wordsworth and Philosophical Necessity", argues that Samuel Taylor Coleridge and William Hazlitt both testified that William Wordsworth in his radical years believed in the doctrine of philosophical necessity. Prompted by that testimony, this essay undertakes a detailed reconstruction of Wordsworth's necessitarianism. Wordsworth was most probably converted to necessity by his reading of William Godwin's *Political Justice*. As a convert to the doctrine in its Godwinian formulation, Wordsworth would have accepted several ideas implicated in the necessitarian infrastructure of *Political Justice*: the human mind's deterministic obligation to reasoned preference, the principle of universal benevolence, a marginalization of human agency and guilt, a prospective approach to ethical questions, and the inevitable triumph of reason and social reform. Wordsworth apparently believed in this complex of ideas only briefly, for the moral pessimism of *Adventures on Salisbury Plain* intimates a lapsing of the poet's Godwinism, including his loss of faith in necessity, by late 1795. By 1797, however, Coleridge allowed Wordsworth to reclaim his necessitarianism by introducing him to an alternate version of the doctrine indebted to Hartleyan associationism and freed from its objectionable Godwinian features. Wordsworth grandly expounds this new version of philosophical necessity in 1798 poetry written for *The Recluse*, but then suddenly seems to lose interest in the idea. In concluding, the essay invokes both Coleridge's 1799 dissatisfaction with necessity and Wordsworth's later writing, especially *The*

*Excursion*, to speculate about the poet's reasons for finally rejecting the doctrine of philosophical necessity in late 1798.[①]

## 2. New Historicism

Maurice Hindle, in "Humphry Davy and William Wordsworth: A Mutual Influence", focuses on the mutual influence between British scientist Humphry Davy and British Romantic poet William Wordsworth. The poetry written by Davy and published in *The Annual Anthology*, edited by Robert Southey, explores how Wordsworth's *Lyrical Ballads* impacted Davy's natural philosophy, and examines how Davy's scientific work on chemistry led Wordsworth to believe there was a creative aspect to science.[②]

Arden Hegele, in "Wordsworth's Dropsy: Flux and Figure in *The Excursion*", traces how William Wordsworth engages with both Romantic medical discourse and aesthetic theory by insisting that the mind is physically embodied and finds his most complex and compelling treatment of this subject in his long poem of 1814, *The Excursion*. Adapting the formal model of poesis as a hydraulic process that he had theorized in the "Preface" to *Lyrical Ballads*, the Wordsworth of 1814 considers minds as embodied brains governed by the influx of both liquid and language: the discovery of a waterlogged Voltaire corresponds to the shape of the Solitary's psychology through the formal mechanisms of intake, excess and outflow. In this poem, however, Wordsworth's well-established hydraulics take on a newly pathological function, as his characters employ the imagery of the dropsy of the

---

[①] Ulmer W A. "William Wordsworth and Philosophical Necessity". Studies in Philology, 2013, 110(1):168-198.

[②] Hindle M. "Humphry Davy and William Wordsworth: A Mutual Influence". Romanticism, 2012, 18(1):16-29.

brain, or hydrocephalus, as they investigate and attempt to treat the Solitary's morbid state of being. What emerges throughout *The Excursion* and, in turn, in "Simon Lee"—is that the physical register of disease stands in for the character's emotional states as a sylleptic structure of feeling. Ultimately, Wordsworth's dropsical brains bring into focus the Romantic idea of poetry as organic form, to ask how mechanistic and organic models might be reconciled in his notion of the hydraulic mind. ①

Kurt Fosso, in "Community and Mourning in William Wordsworth's *The Ruined Cottage*, 1797-1798", examines the attitude of William Wordsworth's attitude of English society as a social structure bound together by, constituted by, and articulated between dead and living, in context of his novel *The Ruined Cottage* of 1797-1798; theme and characterization in the book; conclusion of Kurt on the book. ②

Harold Anthony Lloyd, in "Good Legal Thought: What Wordsworth can Teach Langdell about Forms, Frames, Choices, and Aims", discusses legal analysis in relation to the late poet William Wordsworth's composition of a sonnet on form and the issue, rule, analysis, conclusion (IRAC) case method which was developed by the late jurist Christopher Columbus Langdell. Training for lawyers and law students is addressed, along with choice, the nature and flexibility of framing in thought, and the claim that complete thoughts include reference, issue, analysis, and conclusion (RIAC). ③

Heidi Thomson, in "Wordsworth's *Song for the Wandering Jew* as a Poem for

---

① Hegele A. "Wordsworth's Dropsy: Flux and Figure in *The Excursion*". Romanticism, 2018, 24(1):36-52.

② Fosso K. "Community and Mourning in William Wordsworth's *The Ruined Cottage*, 1797-1798". Studies in Philology, 95, 92(3):329.

③ Lloyd H A. "Good Legal Thought: What Wordsworth can Teach Langdell about Forms, Frames, Choices, and Aims". Vermont Law Review, 2016, 41(1):1-22.

Coleridge", offers poetry criticism of the poem *Song for the Wandering Jew* by William Wordsworth. It states that the poem refers to the ill-treatment of William and Dorothy Wordsworth in Hamburg, Germany. It is noted that the poem is inappropriate for poet Samuel Taylor Coleridge and Wordsworth's book *Lyrical Ballads* as it does not fit in any category. The poem portrays a bond between Wordsworth and Coleridge.①

Jacob Risinger, in "Wordsworth's Imaginative Duty", presents an exploration into the poetry of William Wordsworth and his treatment of literary duty. Several of his poems, especially *Ode to Duty*, are analyzed in regards to his use of the first person and their reflections on his personal aesthetics, career trajectory, and work ethics as a writer. The connections between Wordsworth's idealism and his literary output are particularly examined.②

## 3. Rhetorical Study

Jessica Fay, in "Rhythm and Repetition at Dove Cottage", examines the poetry of William Wordsworth, highlighting his routines and activities at his house Dove Cottage in England. Topics include the characteristics of his poems, the rhythm and repetition in the poems, and his sonnet series "Ecclesiastical Sonnets" on the history of the Church of England. Also discussed are Wordsworth's life at Dove Cottage, his marriage to Dorothy, and their habit of murmuring and humming lines of poetry to themselves.③

Jessica Fay, in "A Question of Loyalty: Wordsworth and the Beaumonts,

---

① Thomson H. "Wordsworth's *Song for the Wandering Jew* as a Poem for Coleridge". Romanticism, 2015, 21(1):37-47.
② Risinger J. "Wordsworth's Imaginative Duty". Romanticism, 2008, 14(3):207-218.
③ Fay J. "Rhythm and Repetition at Dove Cottage". Philological Quarterly, 2018, 97(1):73-95.

Catholic Emancipation and *Ecclesiastical Sketches*", argues in the Roman Catholic Emancipation debate, William Wordsworth took the opposite view to his friend and patron Sir George Beaumont. Whilst Wordsworth's position as a committed anti-emancipationist is well-known, this essay explores the Beaumonts' Catholic heritage and their political allegiances. This contextual material provides a backdrop for a reading of a previously un-noted document that Lady Beaumont sent to the Wordsworths in 1809: "An Account of an English Hermit". This pamphlet, by an unknown Anglican clergyman (Thomas Barnard), describes the life of an unknown nonjuror (Thomas Gardiner). Analysis of the manuscript, and the circumstances of its circulation, resituates Wordsworth's objections to Emancipation and casts new light on the tone of his *Ecclesiastical Sketches* (1822). Jessica explores how Wordsworth uses the "Advertisement" to the sonnets in order to counter any resentment the anti-Catholic publication may have engendered between the poet and Sir George, and conclude with a close reading of "Catechising".[1]

Mark Sandy, in "'Lines of Light': Poetic Variations in Wordsworth, Byron, and Shelley", recognizes the importance of Wordsworth's sense of nascent light (elegised in his *Ode: Intimations of Immortality*), the essay traces how influential this idea was on later Romantic poetic treatments of light. Wordsworth's qualitative distinction between the "fountain light of all our day" and the "light of common day" reveals his alertness to the revelatory and blinding effects of light and establishes the terms of Byron's and Shelley's imaginative engagement with the transformative aspects of light in their depiction of Italian cityscapes and coastal scenes. This transformative quality of light, for Byron and Shelley, is inextricable from those utopian aspirations to recapture future edenic states, which are configured in terms that consign such future idylls to the irrecoverable past. Finally, Shelley's

---

[1] Fay J. "A Question of Loyalty: Wordsworth and the Beaumonts, Catholic Emancipation and *Ecclesiastical Sketches*". Romanticism, 2016, 22(1):1-14.

*The Triumph of Life* is read as avowing an apocalyptic, rather than transformative, light whose "severe excess" is still reimagined in terms familiar to the reader of Wordsworth's "Ode".①

## 4. Canonization Study

Tracy Ware, in "Wordsworth's Canadian Ministries", argues that Canadian writers have long been as divided on the matter of William Wordsworth's influence as writers elsewhere. After looking at the criticism that regards Wordsworth as inappropriate in Canada, this essay considers three aspects of his enduring influence: responses to *I Wandered Lonely as a Cloud*, the preferred text for those who wish to ridicule Wordsworth, but also a touchstone for such poets as Elizabeth Brewster and Don McKay; responses to *Tintern Abbey*, such as Charles G. D. Roberts's *The Tantramar Revisited* and Al Purdy's *The Country North of Belleville*; and Peter Dale Scott's revision of *The Prelude in Minding the Darkness*. Wordsworthian poetry flourishes in diverse environments because it is less a matter of the Lake District than of "the mighty world/Of eye and ear,—both what they half create, /And what perceive" (*Tintern Abbey* 105-107). The essay concludes that Canadian criticism has placed too much emphasis on geography, especially for poets who are not exclusively concerned with national landscapes or themes.②

## 5. Thematic study

David F. Maas, in "Exploring Time-Binding Formulations with William

---

① Sandy M. "'Lines of Light': Poetic Variations in Wordsworth, Byron, and Shelley". Romanticism, 2016, 22(3):260-268.

② Ware T. "Wordsworth's Canadian Ministries". Journal of Canadian Studies, 2013, 47(1):197-220.

Wordsworth", provides information on the time-binding formulations of William Wordsworth; kinds of general semantics formulations anticipated by Wordsworth; advantage of the man's ability to bind time; significance of time-binding. ①

Kurt Fosso, in "A 'World of Shades': Mourning, Poesis, and Community in William Wordsworth's *The Vale of Esthwaite*", discusses races poet William Wordsworth's interpretation of the relationship between the Wordsworthian community, the living and the dead, with specific reference to the poem *The Vale of Esthwaite*. Theme of the poem; how death and mourning are represented in the poem; how the poem's summation of trauma can be represented. ②

Eliza Borkowska, in "'But I am too particular for the limits of my paper': Religion in Wordsworth's Poetry, Prose and Talk", discusses about religious inspiration behind William Wordsworth's poetry focusing on religious subjects or religious imagery that appear in his poetry works including God and Heaven, faith and worship, and Jesus and the Cross. Topics include catholic themes and attitudes in poems, opinion on Catholicism, and topic of worship in Wordsworth's prose. Also discussed are his poems and prose *We are Seven*, *Ode: Intimations of Immortality*, and *The Fenwick notes of William Wordsworth*. ③

Jasmine Jagger, in "Wordsworth, Coleridge, and the Healing Powers of the Imagination", discusses a medical link between Wordsworth and Coleridge during and around the composition of *The Prelude*. Looking closely at popular medical treatises on the imagination and its specific powers over the human mind and body in the late 1700s and early 1800s, it identifies a medical "strand" within *The Prelude*,

---

① Maas D F. "Exploring Time-Binding Formulations with William Wordsworth." A Review of General Semantics, 2004, 61(1):151-158.
② Fosso K. "A 'World of Shades': Mourning, Poesis, and Community in William Wordsworth's *The Vale of Esthwaite*". Modern Language Review, 1998, 93(3):629.
③ Borkowska E. "'But I am too particular for the limits of my paper': Religion in Wordsworth's Poetry, Prose and Talk". Romanticism, 2015, 21(1):14-24.

particularly in relation to its address to an ailing Coleridge. Through biographical tracking and close attention to certain poetic emphases and motifs, it identifies a special motive for Wordsworth's writing of his poem, as well as an emergent dynamic between the two poets at this time: namely, that of benign physician (Wordsworth) and wandering patient (Coleridge).①

## 6. Comparative Study

Stacey McDowell, in "Rhyming and Undeciding in Wordsworth and Norman Nicholson", discusses Wordsworth's poem *Yarrow Unvisited*, suggests that it is better not to go somewhere than to go and risk being disappointed. Responding to this idea in the poem *Askam Unvisited*, the twentieth-century Cumbrian poet Norman Nicholson describes how he had planned to visit the dilapidated town of Askam in the southern Lake District only to face an agony of indecision before resolving in the end not to go. Both poets look forward to a time when they might be forced to look back with regret, and choose instead to preserve a sense of what might have been. A preoccupation with the passage of time and the consequences of decision-making is connected in these poems to the workings of rhyme, particularly to rhyme's relationship with effects of timing and determinism.②

## 7. Reader-Oriented Criticism

Karen Guendel, in "Johnny Foy: Wordsworth's Imaginative Hero", focuses

---

① Jagger J. "Wordsworth, Coleridge, and the Healing Powers of the Imagination". Romanticism, 2016, 22(1):33-47.

② McDowell S. "Rhyming and Undeciding in Wordsworth and Norman Nicholson". Romanticism, 2017, 23(2):179-190.

on William Wordsworth's poem *The Idiot Boy*, which pleasure according to Brooke Hopkins comes from the author's fulfillment of his objective in *Lyrical Ballads* to purify the hearts of his readers. Topics discussed include the criticism of Samuel Taylor Coleridge on Wordsworth's shortcoming in poets' task of giving pleasure in favor of the moral philosopher's search for truth and what kind of poet Johnny represent. ①

Saeko Yoshikawa, in "An 1850 'Wordsworth' Album and the Poet's Nineteenth-Century Reputation", discusses poet William Wordsworth's reputation in the 19th century. Saeko analyzes a mid-Victorian sketch album that was dedicated to the memory of the poet to reveal the fact that many people were very aware of Wordsworth's life before the first biographies about him were written. He attempts to determine the identity of the artist of the album, who was extremely familiar with the places that Wordsworth spent his life. An itinerary of the artist's trips to each destination is presented. ②

## 8. Psychoanalytical Criticism

Mushtaq Rehman and Muhammad Iqbal, in "Wordsworth's Poetry: An Undertone of Psychic Synchronism", argues that humans are consciously torn in the binary opposites; they are not aware that there lies some dark power or psychic twilight working beneath the surface of apparent sharp contradictions that binds the opposites and reconcile them into one organic whole. Wordsworth's poetry, if read from a psychological perspective, manifests such scenes and sights symbolizing these

---

① Guendel K. "Johnny Foy: Wordsworth's Imaginative Hero". Texas Studies in Literature and Language, 2014, 56(1):66-89.
② Yoshikawa S. "An 1850 'Wordsworth' Album and the Poet's Nineteenth-Century Reputation". Romanticism, 2009, 15(2):156-180.

psychic opposites and their psychic integration. This paper is an attempt to psychologically throw light on how these implicit manifestations of psychic integration effectively work in Wordsworth's poetry which carry a message of psychic wholeness for the readers so feverishly involved in outer conflicts and rigid differences disintegrating a vast empire of human society.①

---

① Rehman M, Iqbal M. "Wordsworth's Poetry: An Undertone of Psychic Synchronism". Dialogue, 2014, 9(1):97-103.

# Chapter 6

# Percy Bysshe Shelley

Shelley was born in a wealthy family at Sussex. His father was a conservative man of the landed gentry, and his mother was a beautiful woman. He was a quiet and thoughtful boy. Though gentle by nature, his rebellious qualities were cultivated in his early years. Shelley grew up with violent revolutionary ideas under the influence of the free thinkers, so he held a lifelong aversion to cruelty, injustice, authority, institutional religion and the official shams of respectable society, condemning war, tyranny and exploitation. He is one of the leading romantic poets, an intense and original lyrical poet in the English language. His poems are harder to comprehend than Blake's: imagistically complex, full of classical and mythological allusions. And they also abound in personification and metaphor and other figures of speech which vividly lead to what we see and feel, or resonate to our feelings.

## Critical Perspectives

### 1. New Historicism

Alison Morgan, in "*God Save Our Queen*! Percy Bysshe Shelley and Radical Appropriations of the British National Anthem", discusses the development of the British national anthems *God Save the King* and *God Save the Rights of Man* from the 18th century through the mid 19th century, with a particular focus on the poetry of writer Percy Bysshe Shelley's relationship with the anthem. The influence that British radicals had on British national anthems, including in regard to the political movement of the Jacobites, is discussed.[①]

Eleanor Fitzsimons, in "The Shelleys in Ireland", discusses the experiences of English poet Percy Bysshe Shelley and his wife, Harriet Shelley, in Ireland in 1812 and 1813", and argues that the Shelleys were in Ireland to attempt to assist in the Irish revolutionary movement in Dublin, Ireland. It discusses the contempt that the Shelleys had for then-Chief Secretary for Ireland Lord Castlereagh, their study of Irish history and politics, and the work *An Address to the Irish People* by Percy Bysshe Shelley.[②]

Paul Stock, in "Liberty and Independence: The Shelley-Byron Circle and the State(s) of Europe", discusses the reactions of poets George Gordon Byron, John Cam Hobhouse, and Percy Bysshe Shelley to the political reconstruction of Europe

---

① Morgan A. "*God Save Our Queen*! Percy Bysshe Shelley and Radical Appropriations of the British National Anthem". Romanticism, 2014, 20(1):60-72.

② Fitzsimons E. "The Shelleys in Ireland". History Today, 2014, 64(6):10-16.

after the defeat of Napoleon Bonaparte in 1815. Paul details the poets' understanding of the condition of Europe after decades of ideological and military conflict, with a specific focus on the interpretation of European politics through the use of the words "freedom" and "liberty". Several historical texts are analyzed, including Byron's *Childe Harold's Pilgrimage*. ①

Michael Rossington, in "'The Destinies of the World': Shelley's reception and transmission of European news in 1820-1821", examines the publishing of poetry and other literary works by the English author Percy Bysshe Shelley in response to European news and events through newspapers in the early 1820s. Shelley's utilization of both English speaking newspapers in Italy as well as papers in London, England to carry his politically motivated works to the public is analyzed in detail. ②

Sharon Ruston, in "One of the 'Modern Sceptics': Reappraising Shelley's Medical Education", explores the friendships and intellectual acquaintances English poet Percy Bysshe Shelley made among the Saint Bartholomew's Hospital medical community during the spring of 1811; initial steps Shelley took towards becoming a surgeon himself; context for the science found in *Prometheus Unbound* and later poetry; Shelley's use of a contemporary vocabulary employed within the science of life. ③

## 2. Psychoanalytical Criticism

Merrilees Roberts, in "Psychological Limits in Percy Shelley's Prefaces",

---

① Stock P. "Liberty and Independence: The Shelley-Byron Circle and the State(s) of Europe". Romanticism, 2009, 15(2):121-130.

② Rossington M. "'The Destinies of the World': Shelley's reception and transmission of European news in 1820-1821". Romanticism, 2007, 13(3):233-243.

③ Ruston S. "One of the 'Modern Sceptics': Reappraising Shelley's Medical Education". Romanticism, 2003, 9(1):1.

discusses that the prefaces to Shelley's poems are generally seen as an important addendum to understanding the complex narratorial personae in the poems they accompany; to pull these textual edges into the centre of enquiry allows for consideration of the unique perspectives on ethics and aesthetics that they offer. Merrilees argues that Shelley's prefaces conflate Sympathy conceived of as a personal and morally accountable emotional reflex, such as found in the thought of Adam Smith, and sympathy conceived as the abstract, disinterested aesthetic judgment of Kant's *Critique of Judgment*. This conflation casts the sensitivity of the poet as both a faculty of judgment which forges an only indirect relationship to moral concerns, paradoxically, as something requiring explicitly moral behaviour. This tension engenders a psychological trauma which makes the idea of "the self" a contested, liminal space that marks the edges of Shelley's understanding of the mental operations that occur in aesthetic experience.[①]

Thomas R. Frosch, in "'More than ever can be spoken': Unconscious Fantasy in Shelley's Jane Williams Poems", examines the play of unconscious fantasies of author Percy Bysshe Shelley and his effort to handle them as Shelley in these poems to Jane Williams seeks love, certain types of mastery, and also peace of mind. Peace of mind is a goal not to be undervalued in the troubled, agitated, conflicted psyche that appears throughout his poetry and with particular explicitness and intimacy in these last lyrics. Stuart Curran has seen in the Jane Williams poems an attempt to create a pastoral of the mind and a timeless bower of psychic peace. Williams enters Shelley's poetic mythology in the unfinished *The Zucca*, written in January 1822. In *The Serpent Is Shut Out From Paradise*, also dated January 1822, Shelley writes manifestly about Jane and her husband, Edward Williams, but what he writes about them and exactly whom he is writing for are equivocal. Shelley sent

---

① Roberts M. "Psychological Limits in Percy Shelley's Prefaces". Romanticism, 2018, 24(2): 158-168.

the stanzas to Edward with instructions that he may read them to Jane, but to no one else—and yet Shelley changed his mind and said he would rather not have Edward read the poem to his wife. It seems that Shelley wanted Jane to see the poem but had some conflict about this wish, and that he absolutely did not want his wife, Mary, to see it. ①

Meena Alexander, in "What Use Is Poetry?", discusses the social value of poetry, the psychological analysis of poetry, and the essay "A Defence of Poetry" by Percy Bysshe Shelley, as well as her poem *Question Time*, adapted from an essay by Meena Alexander that was presented to the Yale Political Union in 2013. ②

Barbara Judson, in "Under the Influence: Owenson, Shelley, and the Religion of Dreams", discusses the novel *The Missionary: An Indian Tale*, by Sydney Owenson and particularly focuses on its influence on poet Percy Bysshe Shelley in the realm of dream and desire. Both use dreams and imagery to express political and religious opinions while still appealing to their reader's sensibilities. ③

## 3. Philosophical Study

Daniel E. Lees, in "Berkeley Redux: Imagination as Ethical Power in Shelley's *Mont Blanc*", offers poetry criticism of the poem *Mont Blanc* by Percy Bysshe Shelley. It explores a unified view of life with all phenomena under the control of a single conscious power. Daniel reflects on the post-epiphany seen in the poem's final movement and Shelley's recognition of divine power and his piety in speaking of God. The relationship of reason and imagination to a super-sensible

---

① Frosch T R. "'More than ever can be spoken': Unconscious Fantasy in Shelley's Jane Williams Poems". Studies in Philology, 2005, 102(3):378-413.

② Alexander M. "What Use Is Poetry?". World Literature Today, 2013, 87(5):17-21.

③ Judson B. "Under the Influence: Owenson, Shelley, and the Religion of Dreams". Modern Philology, 2006, 104(2):202-223.

reality is interpreted.[1]

## 4. Deconstruction

Alan Rawes, in "Shelley's 'compelling rhyme schemes' in *The Triumph of Life*", argues that many critics have noted *The Triumph of Life*'s contradictory understandings of "life", interpreting these contradictions as the product of thematic intention or thematic uncertainty. Drawing on a few deconstructive concepts about language and applying these to Shelley's rhymes in *The Triumph of Life*, this essay argues that in Shelley's poem rhymes create and disseminate equivocality of meaning but also offer Shelley a means of engaging creatively with that equivocality, and it is this interplay between form and poet that produces the poem's contradictory readings of "life". It also suggests that paying attention to this interplay working itself out does not just tell us something fundamental about *The Triumph of Life* but also a great deal about Shelley's more general sensitive responsiveness to what he describes in *A Defence of Poetry* as the "relations" between "sounds" and the "uniform and harmonious recurrence of sound", without which poetry, for Shelley, "were not poetry".[2]

## 5. Thematic Study

Betsy Bolton, in "Agency from a Stone: Shelley's Posthumanist Experiments in *Mont Blanc*", reads Shelley's *Mont Blanc* as an extended exploration into

---

[1] Lees D E. "Berkeley Redux: Imagination as Ethical Power in Shelley's *Mont Blanc*". Texas Studies in Literature and Language, 2016, 58(3):278-304.

[2] Rawes A. "Shelley's 'compelling rhyme schemes' in *The Triumph of Life*". Romanticism, 2016, 22(1):76-89.

possible modes of relationship linking the human mind to the material world. The modes of relationship considered by Shelley anticipate many of the structures and strategies developed by posthumanist theory, including structural coupling, strategic anthropomorphism, imagistic translation, and human-nonhuman assemblages. After summarizing Kantian and post-Kantian readings of *Mont Blanc*, the essay works through an extended close reading of the poem to elucidate its proto-posthumanist elements. ①

Christopher Hitt, in "Shelley's Unwriting of *Mont Blanc*", discusses efforts to contribute to the critical discussion of the poem *Mont Blanc* by Percy Bysshe Shelley; analysis of the subject and rhetorical operations of the poem; belief that the poem must be understood in the larger context of literary history; argument that the poem expresses a radical but redemptive skepticism which accepts the otherness of wilderness. ②

## 6. Cultural Study

Michelle Geric, in "Shelley's 'cancelled cycles': Huttonian Geomorphology and Catastrophism in Prometheus Unbound (1819)", discusses a critique of the 1820 poem *Prometheus Unbound* by Percy Byssche Shelley is presented, focusing on its relationship to ideas about earth science, geomorphology, and geological change posited by Scottish geologist James Hutton. It comments on Shelley's conceptions of socio-political and ideological revolution. Hutton's ideas about the earth as self-sustaining and the restorative power of internal heat are considered. Geological

---

① Bolton B. "Agency from a Stone: Shelley's Posthumanist Experiments in *Mont Blanc*". Word and Text, 2016, 6(1):28-47.

② Hitt C. "Shelley's Unwriting of *Mont Blanc*". Texas Studies in Literature and Language, 2005, 47(2):139-166.

catastrophe in the poem is also explored.[1]

## 7. Comparative Study

Matthew Scott, in "'A manner beyond courtesy': Two Concepts of Wonder in Coleridge and Shelley", discusses the notion of wonder in the thought of poets Samuel Taylor Coleridge and Percy Bysshe Shelley, topics include the aesthetic theory espoused by Coleridge, the Elizabethan stage in relation to the aesthetics of playwright William Shakespeare's work, and the definition of poetry in the Romantic thought of Shelley.[2]

---

[1] Geric M. "Shelley's 'cancelled cycles': Huttonian Geomorphology and Catastrophism in Prometheus Unbound (1819)". Romanticism, 2013, 19(1):31-43.

[2] Scott M. "'A manner beyond courtesy': Two Concepts of Wonder in Coleridge and Shelley". Romanticism, 2012, 18(3):227-238.

# Chapter 7

# John Keats

When Keats was eight, his father was killed by a fall from a horse, and when he was fourteen his mother died of tuberculosis. The odes are generally regarded as Keats's most important and mature works. Whatever their subjects are, the poet's abiding preoccupation with imagination always reaches out to unite with the beautiful. Among those works, he also suggests the undercurrent of disillusion that accompanies such ecstasy, the human suffering which forever questions the visionary transcendence achieved by art. The artistic aim of his poetry was to create a beautiful world of imagination as a resist to the sordid reality of his day.

## Critical Perspectives

### 1. New Historicism

Nikki Hessell, in "John Keats and Indian Medicine", argues that John Keats's medical studies at Guy's Hospital coincided with a boom in interest in both the traditional medicines of the sub-continent and the experiences of British doctors and patients in India. Despite extensive scholarship on the impact of Keats's medical knowledge on his poetry, little consideration has been given to Keats's exposure to Indian medicine. The poetry that followed his time at Guy's contains numerous references to the contemporary state of knowledge about India and its medical practices, both past and present. This essay focuses on Isabella and considers the major sources of information about Indian medicine in the Regency. It proposes that some of Keats's medical imagery might be read as a specific response to the debates about medicine in the sub-continent.[①]

Taro Takeuchi, in "Rediscovering the Regency Lute: A Checklist of Musical Sources and Extant Instruments", argues that "Awakening up, he took her hollow lute,—/Tumultuous,—and, in chords that tenderest be,/He played an ancient ditty, long since mute...". These lines from *The Eve of St Agnes*, by John Keats, provide a reminder that the Romantic poets were fascinated by the lute. As if in response, around 1800 an instrument called "lute" or "modern lute" suddenly became fashionable. Most examples had an egg-shaped body, with ten single

---

① Hessell N. "John Keats and Indian Medicine". Romanticism, 2016, 22(2):157-166.

strings, and were built in London by craftsmen such as Buchinger, Barry and Harley. At the same time, older lutes from the 16th and 17th centuries were converted into "modern lutes". This article contributes to a rediscovery of these forgotten lutes and their music in the Regency period. It presents the first census of the nine extant instruments, surveys the original musical sources, and considers matters of playing technique and contemporary instruction books. A surprisingly rich repertory is revealed, for these lutes played arrangements of contemporary popular tunes and dances, but there were also newly composed sonatas, rondos and lute songs. [1]

Richard Cronin, in "Keats and the Double Life of Poetry", argues that Keats, unlike the other Romantics, has prompted not just a dispute as to the character of his political allegiances, but a dispute about whether he is appropriately regarded as a political poet at all. Keats's recent critics are more familiar with the *Poems of 1817* in which Keats emphatically and repeatedly identifies himself as an admiring associate of the editor of *The Examiner*, Leigh Hunt, but even in these poems the ambition to write a poetry that makes its impact on the non-poetic world alternates with a contrary tendency to define the world of the poem by its distance from the world outside it. In the *Poems of 1820* the two tendencies persist, but, instead of working against one another, they allow Keats to resolve his contradictory ambitions and write poems that achieve a formal perfection that releases them from the contingent and yet continue to speak to the contingent world in which we all of us live our lives. [2]

Beth Lau, in "William Godwin and Cockney School Publishing Circles: Leigh Hunt, Charles Ollier, Taylor and Hessey and their Authors, Particularly John

---

[1] Takeuchi T. "Rediscovering the Regency Lute: A Checklist of Musical Sources and Extant Instruments". Early Music, 2018, 46(1):17-34.

[2] Cronin R. "Keats and the Double Life of Poetry". Romanticism, 2016, 22(2):147-156.

Keats", presents on the relationship between author William Godwin and several publishers associated with the so-called Cockney school of writers, including the publishers and booksellers Leigh Hunt, Charles and James Ollier, John Taylor, and James Augustus Hessey. It uses Godwin's diary to explore the connections between several overlapping social networks of authors and publishing firms. Topics discussed include the poets John Keats and Percy Bysshe Shelley.[1]

Stefanie John, in "'Precision Instruments for Dreaming': Anatomizing Keats in Pauline Stainer's *The Wound-dresser's Dream*", examines allusions to Keats in the collection *The Wound-dresser's Dream* (1996) by the contemporary British poet Pauline Stainer. Drawing on the Keatsian notion of dreaming as a metaphor for poetic creativity and responding to Keats as both poet and physician, Stainer explores the interface between sense experience and imagination. As dreams seem to encode hidden meanings, so Stainer's writing evokes the impression that the textual riddles of her poems symbolize greater truths—while the nature of these truths is mostly left unclear. Through extensive use of allusion and surreal, sometimes opaque imagery she foregrounds the status of the poetic work as a linguistic construct. Yet she also maintains a Keatsian belief that poetry's ability to embrace uncertainties and mysteries affords it a unique grasp on actuality.[2]

James Robert Allard, in "Bureaucracy, Pedagogy, Surgery: Keats, Guy's, and the 'Institution' of Medicine", argues that John Keats's time as a medical student provided much fodder for the imagination of readers of all persuasions. In particular, "Z", in the fourth installment of the "Cockney School" essays, took pains to ensure that readers knew of his time training to be an apothecary, working to frame Keats, first, as connected to the lowest branch of medical practice, and,

---

[1] Lau B. "William Godwin and Cockney School Publishing Circles: Leigh Hunt, Charles Ollier, Taylor and Hessey and their Authors, Particularly John Keats". Romanticism, 2011, 17(2):186-194.

[2] John S. "'Precision Instruments for Dreaming': Anatomizing Keats in Pauline Stainer's *The Wound-dresser's Dream*". Romanticism, 2016, 22(2):230-241.

second, as having failed as badly at that unworthy pursuit as he did at poetry. But what would "Z", or any of his readers, have known about the training of an apothecary, about medical pedagogy, about the internal workings of the profession? As outsiders, what could they have known, beyond perception, conjecture, and opinion? And on what were those opinions based? This essay reads "Z"'s comments in the context of first-hand accounts of the state of contemporary medical pedagogy, seeking to account both for "Z"'s dismissal of Keats to "the shops" and for the continuing fascination with his connections to medicine in these terms. [1]

Grant F. Scott, in "New Severn Watercolours from the Voyage to Italy with Keats", rediscovers of three of Joseph Severn's watercolours from his 1820 journey to Italy with Keats, which provides an important visual counterpart to his famous journal-letters. Together with a number of other sketches he made onboard the Maria Crowther, these works offer us a new perspective on the voyage. The watercolours form part of the Charles Lee Smith Papers at Wake Forest University, an archive that also contains other significant Keatsiana, including an inventory of Keats manuscripts and relics which were found in Severn's room after his death. The provenance of the watercolours lends us a fascinating glimpse into the lives of Lady Maureen Watson and her daughters as they flee the threat of Hitler's invasion and try to establish a new life in North Carolina. [2]

Meiko O'Halloran, in "Sage, Humanist, and Physician to All Men: Keats and Romantic Conceptualisations of the Poet", argues that in the aftermath of the French Revolution which failed to give birth to a hoped-for new egalitarian age in Britain, radically-minded poets were forced to confront the question of what their role was in a post-Revolutionary age. This article examines Keats's distinctive

---

[1] Allard J R. "Bureaucracy, Pedagogy, Surgery: Keats, Guy's, and the 'Institution' of Medicine". Romanticism, 2016, 22(2):203-212.

[2] Scott G F. "New Severn Watercolours from the Voyage to Italy with Keats". Romanticism, 2016, 22(2):213-229.

contribution to the debates of his day by exploring his crafting of the figure of the poet in Hyperion and *The Fall of Hyperion*. What do Keats's sympathetic portraits of the fallen Titans and the unrealised perfection of Apollo have to tell us about his conceptions of the poet? Meiko begins by looking back to influential models of the epic poet by Dante, Milton, and Macpherson which Keats and his contemporaries inherited, before examining the extraordinary debate with Moneta in *The Fall of Hyperion* in which the poet-narrator defends the poet as "a sage, /a humanist, physician to all men", only to destabilise his own claim to the title.①

Ou Li, in "Keats, Sextus Empiricus, and Medicine", discusses Keats's affinity with Pyrrhonian scepticism as recorded by Sextus Empiricus in *Outlines of Scepticism* in the following aspects: the investigative, non-dogmatic attitude towards the truth, the ability to set out oppositions and to realise the equipollence in opposed accounts of the truth, suspension of judgement, and the goal of tranquility. It also speculates on the implication of the common medical background Sextus and Keats shared by linking the ethical values of ancient scepticism to the humanitarian concerns of medicine that might have shaped Keats's scepticism. Although the connection between Keats, Sextus, and medicine is speculative, Burton's Anatomy of Melancholy—carefully studied by Keats—mentions Sextus, from which we can assume Keats's exposure to Sextan scepticism. The Renaissance revival of Pyrrhonian scepticism provides us with stronger evidence about its indirect influence on Keats through Montaigne and Shakespeare as its important inheritors.②

Kyoung-Min Han, in "The Urn's 'Silent Form': Keats's Critique of Poetic Judgment", offers criticism on the poem *Ode on a Grecian Urn* by English poet John Keats. He discusses the equation of beauty and truth in the poem as well as the

---

① O'Halloran M. "Sage, Humanist, and Physician to All Men: Keats and Romantic Conceptualisations of the Poet". Romanticism, 2016, 22(2):177-190.

② Li O. "Keats, Sextus Empiricus, and Medicine". Romanticism, 2016, 22(2):167-176.

conflict between sensation and philosophy in the poem. He also explores Keats's philosophical education, focusing on philosophers Immanuel Kant and Gotthold Ephraim Lessing. Also discussed is Keats's use of ekphrasis. ①

## 2. Philosophical Study

Richard C. Sha, in "John Keats and Some Versions of Materiality", presents an examination into the writings of the English Romantic poet John Keats from a materialist perspective. Richard seeks to analyze Keats's aesthetics within the framework of materialist possibility, as opposed to determinism. Further discussion is offered regarding Romantic philosophies of matter and ideals, readdressing their implications on literary aesthetics. ②

## 3. New Criticism

John Barnard, in "Keats's 'Forebodings': Margate, Spring 1817, and After", discusses poet John Keats's writing style or poetic romance focusing on the letters he wrote to essayist Leigh Hunt and painter Benjamin Robert Haydon as he wrote his poem *Endymion* in Margate, England. Topics include Keats's self-representation, use of ironic moments, usage of humor, sexual pun, romance and anti-romance, presentation of female sexuality, and description of state of mind. Several poems by Keats are mentioned like *Sleep and Poetry* and *On the Sea*. ③

---

① Han K M. "The Urn's 'Silent Form': Keats's Critique of Poetic Judgment". Papers on Language & Literature, 2012, 48(3):245-268.
② Sha R C. "John Keats and Some Versions of Materiality". Romanticism, 2014, 20(3):233-245.
③ Barnard J. "Keats's 'Forebodings': Margate, Spring 1817, and After". Romanticism, 2015, 21(1):1-13.

Stacey McDowell, in "Shiftiness in Keats's *Ode on Indolence*", identifies a kind of shiftiness at work in Keats's *Ode on Indolence*. Apparent both in the poem's depiction of indolence as a wavering between mind states, and in its wordplay, ambiguity and structural instability, this shifty quality presents an unsettling, more mischievous side of Negative Capability. This quality may account, too, for the peculiar textual instability of the ode, which has seen the order of its stanzas variously rearranged by critics and editors over the course of its bibliographical history. The essay concludes by considering the indolence of the poem's title in relation to a pun contained in its epigraph, which raises questions about what drives poetic creativity and considers the distinction between the labour of professional authorship versus ideas about inspiration and organic composition.[①]

Gregory Tate, in "Keats, Myth, and the Science of Sympathy", considers the connections between myth and sympathy in Keats's poetic theory and practice. It argues that the *Ode to Psyche* exemplifies the way in which Keats uses mythological narrative, and the related trope of apostrophe, to promote a restrained form of sympathy, which preserves an objectifying distance between the poet and the feelings that his poetry examines. This model of sympathy is informed by Keats's medical training: the influential surgeon Astley Cooper and *The Hospital Pupil's Guide* (1816) both identify a sensitive but restrained sympathy for patients' suffering as an essential part of the scientific and professional methods of nineteenth-century medicine. However, while *The Hospital Pupil's Guide* claims that mythological superstition has been superseded in medicine by positivist science, Keats's ode suggests that myth retains a central role in poetry, as the foundation of a poetic method that mediates between imaginative sympathy and objective impartiality.[②]

---

① McDowell S. "Shiftiness in Keats's *Ode on Indolence*". Romanticism, 2017, 23(1):27-37.
② Tate G. "Keats, Myth, and the Science of Sympathy". Romanticism, 2016, 22(2):191-202.

Robert K. Lapp, in "Authorship in *Eighteen Hundred and Eleven*: An Integral Approach", discusses the authorship in 1811 citing reference to the romantic poetry of John Keats, William Wordsworth, and Samuel Taylor Coleridge; a critical approach derived from the Integral Theory of philosopher Ken Wilber that refocuses the understanding of the author function in general; the articulation of the authorship of poet Anna Laetitia Barbauld in the poem *Eighteen Hundred and Eleven*. ①

## 4. Canonization Study

David Havird, in "'Passion Before We Die': James Dickey and Keats", discusses the way American poet and novelist James Dickey was inspired by the work by English Romantic poet John Keats, who believes that the world is a vale of Soul-making. Dickey described Keats as one of the great human presence in the whole of history in his 1968 commencement address at the University of Carolina. David says Dickey's *May Day Sermon* could be a retelling of Keats's *The Eve of St. Agnes*, despite him claiming that it is a retelling of a local folk myth. In *The Sheep Child* considered as his most notorious poem, Dickey profanely subverts the idea contained in Keats's *Ode on a Grecian Urn*. ②

## 5. Reader-Oriented Criticism

Alexandra Paterson, in "'A Greater Luxury': Keats's Depictions of Mistiness and Reading", discusses depictions of mist or mistiness in the poetry of poet John

---

① Lapp R K. "Authorship in *Eighteen Hundred and Eleven*: An Integral Approach". English Studies in Canada, 2012, 38(2):49-70.

② Havird D. "'Passion Before We Die': James Dickey and Keats". The Southern Literary Journal, 2013, 45(2):90-102.

Keats as it relates to the experience of reading. Topics include the use of the term mist in the poem *Paradise Lost*, by John Milton, its use in Keats's poem *Ode to a Nightingale*, and an 1818 letter from Keats to poet John Hamilton Reynolds. Also noted are Keats's sonnet *On First Looking Into Chapman's Homer*, the role of a Muse in an 1818 sonnet by Keats, and the relationship between hearing and seeing in Keats's work.[①]

---

① Paterson A. "'A Greater Luxury': Keats's Depictions of Mistiness and Reading". Romanticism, 2012, 18(3):260-269.

# Chapter 8

# Alfred Lord Tennyson

Alfred is the fourth son in a family of twelve children. He is certainly the most representative, Victorian poet. His poetry voices the doubt and the faith, the grief and the joy of the English people in an era of fast social changes. Tennyson is a great Victorian poet conscious of the situation of his age. He is the first major writer to reveal the perception of the vast extent of geological time that has haunted human consciousness since Victorian scientists exposed the history of the Earth's crust. Tennyson has the natural power of linking visual pictures with musical expressions, and with strong feelings. He also has perfect control of the sound of English, and a sensitive ear, an excellent choice of words. His poetry is rich in poetic images and melodious language, and noted for its lyrical beauty and metrical charm. His works are not only the products of the creative imagination of a poetic genius but also products of a long and rich English heritage. His wonderful works manifest all the qualities of England's great poets.

## Critical Perspectives

### 1. Comparative Study

Ebtihal Elshaikh, in "Dialogical Self in Tennyson's *Ulysses* and Farooq Guwaida's *A Star Looking for an Orbit*", argues that Dialogical Self Theory sees the self as a complex system consisting of several other selves or "I-positions". The theory is an important technique to study the narrative discourse, especially in literary genres like drama and novel; but rarely applied to poetry. The aim of this paper is to apply the theory of Dialogical Self to two poems: *Ulysses* by Alfred Lord Tennyson, and *A Star Looking for an Orbit* by Farooq Guwaida. The paper is going to discuss how these two writers use two mythical figures that have much in common, Ulysses and Sinbad, to represent two different experiences of Victorian England and Postmodern Egypt. Both writers reflect the psychological conflict and the identity crisis that are the outcome of such societies at crossroads. In *Ulysses* and *A Star Looking for an Orbit*, we face a multi-layered identity, or what Hermans calls different I-positions in a dialogue with each other. Tennyson is known to be one of the speakers of the Victorian age. His poetry comes to reflect the Victorian interests and issues. In his poem, *Ulysses*, Tennyson expresses, through his use of the Greek myth of Ulysses, the social and political dilemma of the Victorian society and the conflict that rises between an individual identity and a social one. Throughout the poem we confront many I-positions that represent Tennyson's self and his contemporary culture. Guwaida, likewise, and through his use of the oriental myth of Sinbad, represents the psychological conflict that tears the contemporary Egyptian self apart. The I-positions that we meet in Guwaida reflect the difficulty of dialogue between the two realms of the poet's self: the external realm representing the harsh postmodern reality, and the internal realm representing the adventurous romantic self. ①

Christina Henderson, in "A Nation of the Continual Present: Timrod, Tennyson, and the Memorialization of the Confederacy", discusses the connections in the works of American poet Henry Timrod and Alfred, Lord Tennyson. Maud Dickson, in his 1886 article, described Timrod as the Tennyson of South Carolina while in a 1893 *The Sewanee Review* by Henry E. Shepherd, Timrod's writing was compared to that of Tennyson in the latter's *In Memoriam*. Timrod's version of Arthur's Knights of the Round Table follows the same formula as the southern warriors also do observe a code of behavior like honor and truth without stain, which echoes the values in Tennyson's work. According to Christina, the works of Timrod speak on behalf of the white South and immortalize not only himself, but also his South. ②

## 2. Poststructuralism

Timuçin Buğra Edman, in "Power in Jeopardy: A Poststructuralist Reading of the Arthurian Legend from Malory's *Le Morte d'Arthur* and Tennyson's *Idylls of the King* to Tolkien's *The Lord of the Rings*", discusses that the days of the classical heroes are over, as the days of romance or chivalric romance and epic that depict the hero in quest of the ideal are. A typical romance situates the hero in a succession of

---

① Elshaikh E. "Dialogical Self in Tennyson's *Ulysses* and Farooq Guwaida's *A Star Looking for an Orbit*". The International Journal of Interdisciplinary Social Sciences, 2010, 5(9):393-404.

② Henderson C. "A Nation of the Continual Present: Timrod, Tennyson, and the Memorialization of the Confederacy". The Southern Literary Journal, 2013, 45(2):19-38.

challenges, each of which is overcome by him, who finally defeats the dark, evil force and brings peace and order to his community, thus offering to it the opportunity of living in a system defined by the norms of universal morality and enlightenment. The hero becomes a model of universal justice and stability, and he towers above all of his fellow men as a symbol of perfection and endurance of will against the powers of darkness. This plot of one-man challenge and task has been much fruitful in the creation of the stories of the pre-Christian times, the times of the foundation and expansion of Christianity, and the Medieval Age. During these eras such legendary figures as Osiris, Prometheus, Moses, Jesus Christ, and King Arthur of England have emerged as representative perfect super heroes and as universal and absolute role models. Known as monomyths, such stories have shown parallelism regarding the character and plot structure, all yielding similarities as dictated by Romance; this is mostly obvious through the continuous clash of good and evil. The clash creates a sustained tension in the reader whose moral understanding and conscience are kept busy in wondering whether the hero will lose the battle of righteousness or win it, announcing that human dignity has once again been victorious over evil forces. As suggested above, the days of such heroes are over, together with their references to super human qualities which have long been referred to as universal symbols that stand for ideal models for humanity. Such symbols, signifiers, refer to a sign both in Semiotics and Linguistics. Simply, it can be defined as something which has a meaning other than itself. Therefore, conventionally, a sign is assumed to transmit information to the one who understands or deciphers it and signified elements. Signifiers intended or ultimate logos to be reflected through signifiers have become clichés. Henceforth, this situation hinders the creativity of the contemporary writer, John Ronald Reuel Tolkien, who has experienced both modernism and postmodernism. An updated deconstruction of romance and epic and their referents by J. R. R. Tolkien in his *The Lord of the*

*Rings* is a strong anti-thesis of the old principles of authorship. The signifiers Tolkien uses do not yield a single conventional signified, although they refer to the sub-creation, in which unique characters and events were created in a peculiar world, that is, Middle-earth. Besides, Tolkien, inspired by Camelot and the Arthurian legends of both Sir Thomas Malory's *Le Morte d'Arthur* and Alfred, Lord Tennyson's *Idylls of the King*, deconstructs the conventional signifiers in his works. [1]

## 3. Psychoanalytical Criticism

Andrew Hamilton, in "On Remembering Poems", discusses the potential challenges and benefits of remembering poetry, whether correctly or with difficulty, focusing on his experiences remembering poems from poets such as Alfred Lord Tennyson, Walt Kelly, and Ogden Nash. Topics include poems about aging and poems such as *The Final Soliloquy of the Interior Paramour*, by Wallace Stevens. [2]

## 4. New Historicism

Allison Adler Kroll, in "Tennyson and the Metaphysics of Material Culture: The Early Poetry", presents an exploration into the early poetry of Alfred Lord Tennyson and its engagement with contemporary 19th-century debate over material culture and the preservation of the cultural past in England. Poems cited and

---

[1] Edman T B. "Power in Jeopardy: A Poststructuralist Reading of the Arthurian Legend from Malory's *Le Morte d'Arthur* and Tennyson's *Idylls of the King* to Tolkien's *The Lord of the Rings*". Journal of History, Culture and Art Research, 2015, 4(2):88-102.

[2] Hamilton A. "On Remembering Poems". New Criterion, 2013, 31(10):88-90.

analyzed regarding their thematic discussion of memory, relics, and the metaphysics of history include *Le Morte d'Arthur*, *Nothing Will Die*, and *Ode to Memory*.①

## 5. Narratology Study

Veronica Forrest-Thomson, in "Pastoral and Elegy in the Early Poems of Tennyson", presents an attempt to come to terms with aspects of English poet William Empson's thought. It also identifies Lord Alfred Tennyson's neglected early poetry a curious combination of pastoral with elegy. Tennyson argues that this invented genre enables a distinctive kind of "fictionalization" in which landscape and object and character tend to blur. Elegiac pastoral transforms directed grief into generalized mood.②

Jerome J. Mcgann, in "Literature by Design since 1790", explores the role of design in 18th and 19th century poetry. It notes the control exercised by poet William Blake through creating the books entirely by himself, poet Emily Dickinson's equally total control through refusal to publish, poet Walt Whitman's close involvement with printers, and the interest of Alfred Lord Tennyson in the look of his poems in print. Poems by Dickinson, Whitman and Tennyson are analyzed for the role of textual design in their meanings.③

## 6. Canonization Study

Ben Glaser, in "Polymetrical Dissonance: Tennyson, A. Mary F. Robinson,

---

① Kroll A A. "Tennyson and the Metaphysics of Material Culture: The Early Poetry". Victorian Poetry, 2009, 47(3):461-480.

② Forrest-Thomson V. "Pastoral and Elegy in the Early Poems of Tennyson". Chicago Review, 2011, 56(2/3):48-76.

③ Mcgann J J. "Literature by Design since 1790". Victorian Poetry, 2010, 48(1):11-40.

and Classical Meter", discusses how the Greek translator A. Mary F. Robinson influenced the use of meter in English poetry through her research of Greek poetry. The experimental poetry of Alfred Lord Tennyson, in which he played with quantitative verse, is also examined. The versification that Robinson used in her 1881 translation of the play *Hippolytus*, by Euripides, is explored. Tennyson's poem *De Profundis* is also analyzed in terms of its use of meter. [1]

---

[1] Glaser B. "Polymetrical Dissonance: Tennyson, A. Mary F. Robinson, and Classical Meter". Victorian Poetry, 2011, 49(2):199-216.

# Chapter 9
# Robert Browning

The personal life of Robert Browning falls into three phases: his years as a child and young bachelor, as a husband, and as a widower. Each of these phases is appropriately considered in relation to his development as a poet. The dramatic monologue, as Browning uses it, separates the speaker from the poet in such a way that the reader must work through the words of the speaker to discover the meaning of the poet. In addition to his experiments with the dramatic monologue, Browning also experimented with language and syntax. The grotesque rhymes and jaw-breaking diction that he often employs have been repugnant to some critics. Still, Browning's poetry that separates it from the Victorian age is its style. Browning draws from a different tradition, more colloquial and discordant, a tradition that includes the poetry of John Donne, the soliloquies of Shakespeare, the comic verse of the early nineteenth-century poet Thomas Hood, and certain features of the narrative style of Chaucer. Browning's role as a forerunner of twentieth-century literature is compatible with his essential Victorianism Energy and perhaps the most characteristic aspect of his writing and of the man. And energy is perhaps the most characteristic aspect of Victorian literature in general. Often, of course, such energy was misdirected. However, such buoyancy is a virtue imparting a creative vitality to all of Browning's writing.

## Critical Perspectives

## 1. New Historicism

Jennifer McDonell, in "Henry James, Literary Fame, and the Problem of Robert Browning", examines Robert Browning's and Henry James's writings to consider their responses to, and implication in, the production, circulation, and consumption of late nineteenth-century celebrity. For James, there were two Brownings—the private, unknowable genius and the social personality. From the time he first met Browning until 1912, James held to this theory in letters, essays, biography, and fiction; the Browning "problem" became integral to James's fascinated engagement with other problems at the heart of celebrity culture. Both writers attacked celebrity discourses and practices (biography, interviews, literary tourism) that constructed the life as a vital source of meaning, thus threatening to displace the writer's work as privileged object of literary interpretation. Browning preceded James in insisting that the separation of public and private life was foundational to an impersonal aesthetics, and in exploring the fatal confusion between art and life that has been identified by theorists as central to celebrity culture.[①]

Oliver Wort, in "Staging *Fra Lippo Lippi*", discusses the poem *Fra Lippo Lippi* by Robert Browning and examines the dramatic aspects of it based on theater director Edward Gordon Craig's interest in adapting the poem into a performance piece. It

---

① McDonell J. "Henry James, Literary Fame, and the Problem of Robert Browning". Critical Survey, 2015, 27(3):43-62.

looks at how Craig perceived Browning's dramatic imagination through the monologue of *Fra Lippo Lippi*. ①

Laura H. Clarke, in "Gathering Sense from Song: Robert Browning and the Romantic Epistemology of Music", presents a criticism of the 19th century English poetry of Robert Browning. She discusses the role of music in Browning's poetry, the influence of German romanticism on music, and the impact of German philosophy Arthur Schopenhauer on the epistemological aspects of Browning's poetry. ②

## 2. Ethical Study

Emily Walker Heady, in "Robert Browning, Theologian: The Incarnational Politics of *Fra Lippo Lippi*", explores the use by 19th century poet Robert Browning of the doctrine of Incarnation in the poem *Fra Lippo Lippi* to highlight the intersections between aesthetics and ethics. Topics discussed include the connection between Browning's work and the doctrine of Incarnation, the rejection of the claim that art should elevate the mind above the physical world and the difficulties of an incarnational artistic and religious praxis. ③

## 3. New Criticism

Amy R. Wong, in "Town Talk and the Cause Célèbre of Robert Browning's *The Ring and the Book*", presents describing the town talkers of late seventeenth

---

① Wort O. "Staging *Fra Lippo Lippi*". Victorian Poetry, 2018, 56(4):413-431.
② Clarke L H. "Gathering Sense from Song: Robert Browning and the Romantic Epistemology of Music". Victorian Poetry, 2017, 55(4):471-494.
③ Heady E W. "Robert Browning, Theologian: The Incarnational Politics of *Fra Lippo Lippi*". Renascence, 2015, 67(2):147-160.

century within the poem *The Ring and the Book* of English poet Robert Browning. Amy discusses the central functions of town talk within the poem towards Browning's own words. He examines the ways that repetition of the types of town talk within the poem in 1860s media forms.①

## 4. Thematic Study

Alison Chapman, in "Robert Browning's Homesickness", presents on the poem *Home-Thoughts, from Abroad* by the Victorian poet Robert Browning. The essay discusses the interrogative nature of the poem, the relationship between the country of England and Europe as expressed in the poem and the poem as a dramatic monologue. Alison makes the claim that the poem parodies both patriotism and lyricism.②

## 5. Narratology Study

Linda H. Peterson, in "Robert Browning's Debut: Ambition Expressed, Ambition Denied", presents on the Victorian poet and playwright Robert Browning. The essay discusses Browning's poetic debut with the poem *Pauline* in 1833 and Browning's ambition as demonstrated by his inclusion of an epigraph from the poet *Clément Marot* in his first publication, as well as a preface by astrologist Cornelius Agrippa. The essay also provides an analysis of the poem and discusses the significance of the paratexts of the poem and the publisher, Saunders and Otley.③

---

① Wong A R. "Town Talk and the Cause Célèbre of Robert Browning's *The Ring and the Book*". Modern Philology, 2016, 113(4):550-572.
② Chapman A. "Robert Browning's Homesickness". Victorian Poetry, 2012, 50(4):469-484.
③ Peterson L H. "Robert Browning's Debut: Ambition Expressed, Ambition Denied". Victorian Poetry, 2012, 50(4):451-468.

Ashby Bland Crowder, in "Attribution and Misattribution: New Poems by Robert Browning?", presents on the confusion surrounding what poet Robert Browning wrote and did not write as a result of being married to a poet like himself. It attempts to sort through some of these problems of attribution and reclaims two poems for Robert Browning. It also argues that nine poems are possibly his and proposes the acceptance of his authorship of a newly-found poem, *To Caroline. —A Lover's Oath*. [1]

Britta Martens, in "'Hardly Shall I Tell My Joys and Sorrows': Robert Browning's Engagement with Elizabeth Barrett Browning's Poetics", focuses on the poetic styles of poets Robert Browning and Elizabeth Barrett Browning (EBB). While the courtship correspondence has long been recognized as the private locus for the couple's dialogue on their respective poetic styles, critics have failed to discern the pursuit by Browning of the same "dialogue" within a number of his own poems. Browning assumes that poetry can, at least in EBB's case, act as a quasi-transparent means of self-expression, while he considers himself as yet unable to reveal his self in his poetry. All three poems analyzed have shown Browning experimenting with the personal mode, making the literary text an arena for playing out the oppositions between EBB's and his own irreconcilable poetics. [2]

Patricia Rigg, in "Augusta Webster, Dramatic Forms, and the Religious Aesthetic of Robert Browning's *The Ring and the Book*", presents a critique of the narrative poem *The Ring and the Book*, by Robert Browning, focusing on the themes of dramatic form, religious aesthetics, and the influence of the contemporary poet Augusta Webster. Topics addressed include an overview of the professional relationship between Webster and Browning, the art of characterization through the

---

[1] Crowder A B. "Attribution and Misattribution: New Poems by Robert Browning?". Philological Quarterly, 2012, 91(3):443-464.

[2] Martens B. "'Hardly Shall I Tell My Joys and Sorrows': Robert Browning's Engagement with Elizabeth Barrett Browning's Poetics". Victorian Poetry, 2005, 43(1):75-97.

melodrama and monologue forms, and the poem's depiction of the religious characters of Pompilia and Jeanne.[1]

## 6. New Criticism

Peter Merchant, in "Winking through the Chinks: Eros and Ellipsis in Robert Browning's *Love among the Ruins*", discusses "Robert Browning's poem *Love among the Ruins*, the idea that the end is actually a starting point is examined. Peter goes on to look at love in further detail, its relation to the last line of the poem, and explains that although one expects the poem to come to an end it actually conveys the feeling of irresolution. The idea of an ellipsis is also discussed.[2]

Olivia Loksing Moy, in "Simian, Amphibian, and Able: Reevaluating Browning's Caliban", analyzes the poem *Caliban upon Setebos; or, Natural Theology in the Island* by British poet Robert Browning is presented. It uses new formalism and disability studies approach to examine how the physical form of the Caliban in the poem reflects Browning's conceptions of poetic meaning, ability and disability, and imaginative power.[3]

## 7. Psychoanalytical Criticism

Linda M. Shires, in "Hardy's Browning: Refashioning the Lyric", presents on the Victorian poets Robert Browning and Thomas Hardy. The essay discusses

---

[1] Rigg P. "Augusta Webster, Dramatic Forms, and the Religious Aesthetic of Robert Browning's *The Ring and the Book*". Victorian Poetry, 2015, 53(1):1-14.

[2] Merchant P. "Winking through the Chinks: Eros and Ellipsis in Robert Browning's *Love among the Ruins*". Victorian Poetry, 2007, 45(4):349-368.

[3] Moy O L. "Simian, Amphibian, and Able: Reevaluating Browning's Caliban". Victorian Poetry, 2018, 56(4):381-411.

Browning's influence on Hardy, the elements of case logic, role play and the discourse of interruption in the lyric poetry of Hardy as well as offers an analysis of poems by the two men. The essay argues that the foundation of Browning's poetry helped Hardy to alter the future of the lyric. ①

---

① Shires L M. "Hardy's Browning: Refashioning the Lyric". Victorian Poetry, 2012, 50(4):583-603.

# Chapter 10

# William Butler Yeats

William Butler Yeats was born in Sandymount, Dublin. His father's family, of English stock, had been in Ireland for at least 200 years; his mother's, the Pollexfens, hailing originally from Devon, had been for some generations in Silgo, in the west of Ireland. Yeats did not like the aesthetic idea of "art for art's sake". To write about Ireland for an Irish audience and to recreate a specifically Irish literature—these were aims that Yeats was fighting for as a poet and a playwright. Yeats had a very long poetic career, from the 1880s to the 1930s. His career coincided with the development of modern history and the disintegration of social values and human beliefs which had a great impact both on techniques and subject matter of modern literature. Yeats is rather a poet of man than nature. With Yeats, poetry is life. His poems tend to present human life in the mode of drama and conflicts in place and time with the value residing in the conflict rather than in the final victory. His characteristic poems are cries, laments, prayers, legends, and rebukes; they are human sound rather than objects. When he died in January 1939, he left a body of verse that, in variety and power, made him beyond question the greatest twentieth-century poet of English.

## Critical Perspectives

## 1. Narratology Study

Raşit Çolark, in "Paratextual Comparison of Two Poets: William Butler Yeats and Avnî", argues that William Butler Yeats is an Irish writer, dramatist, educationist and philosopher. Sultan Mehmed II, the Conqueror of Istanbul, is one of the greatest sultans of the Ottoman Empire. W. B. Yeats was born in Ireland on 13th of June in 1865 and he died on 28th of January in 1939 in France. Sultan Mehmed II was born at Edirne Palace on 30th of March, in 1432 and he died on the 3rd of May in 1481 in Istanbul. Despite the fact that they originated from different societies and nations, they wrote poems about similar themes such as nation, land, freedom and love. In this study, it is expected to research Irish statesman, William Butler Yeats who won the Noble prize for literature in 1923 and Mehmed II who conquered Istanbul in 1453 and wrote various ghazals by comparing the books *Fâtih Dîvânı ve Şerhi* translated in English as Diwan of Sultan Mehmed II with Commentary and *The Collected Works of William Butler Yeats* Volume I whose subtitle is *The Poems* through paratextuality. Paratextual approach which belongs to French literary critic Gérard Genette is going to be the main agent in assessing life, works and impressions of both extraordinary artists, Archpoet and Avnî.[①]

Nadezhda V. Petrunina, in "Esoteric Metaphors in W. B. Yeats's Early Poetry and Its Russian Translations", dwells on idio-style of William Butler Yeats,

---

① Çolark R. "Paratextual Comparison of Two Poets: William Butler Yeats and Avnî". Journal of Graduate School of Social Sciences, 2019, 23(2):675-683.

a renowned Anglo-Irish poet, famous for his interest in esoteric doctrines. Topics analyzed are the influence of several esoteric motifs on the stylistic device of metaphor employed by the poet and the specificity of the metaphorical contexts in the Russian translations of Yeats's verse. [1]

## 2. Cultural Study

Bernard McKenna, in "Yeats, *On the Boiler*, the Aesthetics of Cultural Disintegration and the Program for Renewal 'of our own rich experience'", argues that in *On the Boiler*, W. B. Yeats depicts the collapse of his paradigm for Ireland's renewal through culture and discerns the seeds for a new cultural movement rooted in education and eugenics. Through education and eugenics, Yeats foresees the rebirth of a new paradigm of cultural nationalism engendered in the "rich experience" of the Irish people and achieving an end very much akin to his earlier paradigm, with a significant addition: Yeats thought to extend his program for cultural renewal beyond the grave. He hoped to foster, through education and eugenics, a like-minded community of believers who would be able to enter into communion with the spirits of men of genius, including himself. [2]

Rob Doggett, in "Aristocratic Patronage and the Commercial Logic of Yeats's *Responsibilities*", challenges the longstanding critical assumption that the poems in W. B. Yeats's *Responsibilities* (1914) offer a categorical rejection of modern consumer society. Although Yeats is clearly disdainful of middle-class culture and nostalgic for a pre-modern community unified by the arts, the poems, Rob argues,

---

[1] Petrunina N V. "Esoteric Metaphors in W. B. Yeats' Early Poetry and Its Russian Translations". European Researcher, 2013, 39(1-2):169-174.

[2] McKenna B. "Yeats, *On the Boiler*, the Aesthetics of Cultural Disintegration and the Program for Renewal 'of our own rich experience'". Journal of Modern Literature, 2012, 35(4):73-90.

strategically exploit the logic of the modern marketplace. By looking at the poems in rhetorical terms, as cultural productions designed to convince people in the present to spend money on the proposed Hugh Lane Gallery of Modern Art, Rob suggests that Yeats exploits commercial logic in three specific ways: by associating mundane consumer exchange with hoarding, as if the true capitalist is a miser; by tapping into the modern advertising strategy of equating choice of purchases with self-worth; and by rendering the object for purchase in abstract terms, such that the "product", again in good advertising fashion, always promises something more than it can deliver. ①

## 3. New Historicism

Daniel Spoth, in "The House that Time Built: Structuring History in Faulkner and Yeats", recounts, briefly, the affinities that previous critics have drawn between William Faulkner and William Butler Yeats, and suggests their shared architectural sensibility as a new medium for assessing their individual literary consciousnesses in parallel. This sensibility finds play in the Big Houses of both of these authors' works: *Sutpen's Hundred in Absalom, Absalom*! and the 'marvelous empty sea-shell' of the palatial manor in Yeats's *Meditations in Time of Civil War*. The anxiety surrounding these structures' potential destruction in both of these authors' works, Daniel argues, is less directed towards the threat of their physical annihilation than towards the dialectic model of history itself: the threat of destroying the house becomes the threat of destroying the very notion of teleology, of effacing the structural sum of history. Daniel performs separate studies of two Big Houses from which these authors drew their architectural inspiration: for Faulkner,

---

① Doggett R. "Aristocratic Patronage and the Commercial Logic of Yeats's *Responsibilities*". Journal of Modern Literature, 2010:1-18.

Rowan Oak in Oxford, MS and for Yeats, Lissadell in County Sligo, Ireland. The manners in which these houses grant and restrict access to their occupants, Daniel argues, suggest ideals that are more divergent than these authors' mutual anxieties, the mutual and manifold hybridities of their domestic spaces, might indicate. ①

## 4. Postcolonial Studies

Ioana Mohor-Ivan, in "Envisaging a Post-colonial Theatre: W. B. Yeats and the Cuchulain Cycle of Plays", starts from Edward Said's and claims that W. B. Yeats's work should be seen as seminal in the process of Ireland's decolonisation, despite the artist's Ascendancy roots and Protestant sympathies, the paper focuses on the Yeatsian theatre as exemplified by the five plays which cluster around the figure of the Celtic hero Cuchulain (*On Baile's Strand*, *The Golden Helmet*, *At The Hawk's Well*, *The Only Jealousy of Emer*, and *The Death of Cuchulain*) in order to prove that the hybrid dramatic forms adopted by Yeats, which rework the Celtic myth within Greek and Japanese theatrical models, may be seen as a move away from "the regional nativism" characteristic of much of the Revival writings towards a "radically liberating" (Deane 1990: 5) vision on a "contaminated" culture, characterised by plurality and dialogism. As such, the Cuchulain cycle of plays may be read not only as a reflection of the Yeatsian decolonising project, but also as an early instance of a postcolonial drama, whose hybrid paradigm subverts and revaluates both imperialist and nationalist assumptions on essentialist notions of identity. ②

---

① Spoth D. "The House that Time Built: Structuring History in Faulkner and Yeats". European Journal of American Culture, 2007, 26(2):109-126.
② Mohor-Ivan I. "Envisaging a Post-colonial Theatre: W. B. Yeats and the Cuchulain Cycle of Plays". Cultural Intertexts, 2016, 5:102-111.

## 5. Philosophical Study

David Dwan, in "Yeats, Heidegger and the Problem of Modern Subjectivism", discusses how William Butler Yeats's early poetic and political trajectory may be viewed as an attempt to engage with and emerge from what Martin Heidegger termed the modern metaphysics of subjectivity. Concept of tradition that Yeats challenges modern subjectivism; Heidegger's criticism of the dominance of the spectator-model in philosophy.[1]

---

[1] Dwan D. "Yeats, Heidegger and the Problem of Modern Subjectivism". Paragraph, 2002, 25(1):74-91.

# Part II  American Poets

# Chapter 11

# Emily Dickinson

Emily Dickinson was born on December 10, 1830, in Amherst, Massachusetts, the second child of Emily Norcross Dickinson and Edward Dickinson. Economically, politically, and intellectually, the Dickinsons was one of Amherst's most prominent families. With her formal experimentation and bold thematic ambitions, Emily Dickinson is recognized as one of the greatest American poets, a poet who continues to exert an enormous influence on the way writers think about the possibilities of poetic craft and vocation. It is sometimes possible to extract autobiography from her poems, but she was not a confessional poet, rather, she used personae—invented first-person speakers—to dramatize the various situation, moods, and perspectives she explored to her lyrics. Though each of her poems is individually short, when collected in one volume, her nearly eighteen hundred surviving poems( she probably wrote hundreds more that were lost) have the feel of an epic produced by the one who devoted much of her life to art.

## Critical Perspectives

### 1. Comparative Study

Marissa Grunes, in "Open Interiority: Emily Dickinson, Augustine, and the Spatial Self", focuses on paradoxes, doubling, and fragmentation of the self in Emily Dickinson's poetry have given rise to significant debate within Dickinson criticism. It mentions secular view of her self-division is plagued by charges of anachronism and speculative analysis and influence embraces both secular and spiritual traditions of self division and self-discovery. It also mentions spatial paradox and architectural metaphors of Augustine's writing and limits of language.①

### 2. New Historicism

Midori Asahina, in "Reconsidering Mabel Loomis Todd's Role in Promoting Emily Dickinson's Writings", focuses on reconsideration of the role of Mabel Loomis Todd in promoting the writings of poet Emily Dickinson and contains poems with no original manuscripts extant. It mentions editorial amity between Susan Dickinson and Mabel Loomis Todd and their partisans and bindings of important units of the poems called fascicles as a part of creative editing. It also mentions

---

① Grunes M. "Open Interiority: Emily Dickinson, Augustine, and the Spatial Self". Women's Studies, 2018, 47(3):350-371.

Todd recognized her artistry and worked to promote appreciation of the poet. [1]

Neil Soderstrom, in "A Poet's GIFTS", discusses the restoration of American poet Emily Dickinson's conservatory that offers new perspective on her daily life and creative process. It mentions the addition of The Evergreens house and The Homestead contingent as part of the Emily Dickinson Museum, which occupies north of Main Street and includes the family orchard and gardens. The identification of Daphne odora and jasmine among the favorites of Dickinson as they were among the first to bloom in winter is also tackled. [2]

Jason Hoppe, in "Personality and Poetic Election in the Preceptual Relationship of Emily Dickinson and Thomas Wentworth Higginson, 1862-1886", presents on the preceptual relationship of poet Emily Dickinson with author Thomas Wentworth Higginson. This relationship is reflected in Dickinson's letters to Higginson and the poem *Image of Light*. Jason examines the absence of an elaboration of the preceptor's knowledge of the scholar's course of study. He claims that their relationship supposes the inseparability of literary endeavor from a manner of micro social intercourse. [3]

## 3. Canonization Study

Claire Nashar, in "Their Conceptual Dickinson: Emily Dickinson in the Work of Tan Lin and a. j. carruthers", focuses on popularity of poetic avant-garde of poet Emily Dickinson and exceptional formal inventiveness and intellectual vibrancy of

---

[1] Asahina M. "Reconsidering Mabel Loomis Todd's Role in Promoting Emily Dickinson's Writings". Women's Studies, 2018, 47(3):302-316.

[2] Soderstrom N. "A Poet's GIFTS". Horticulture, 2018, 115(1):46-51.

[3] Hoppe J. "Personality and Poetic Election in the Preceptual Relationship of Emily Dickinson and Thomas Wentworth Higginson, 1862-1886". Texas Studies in Literature and Language, 2013, 55(3): 348-387.

her poems. Topics discussed include concerns of contemporary conceptual poetics with mutability of genre, and textual consumption, self-theorized movement in early twenty-first-century Anglophone poetics and optical character recognition (OCR) technology into machine-encoded text. ①

## 4. Philosophical Study

Yanbin Kang, in "Dickinson's Air/Wind: 'Lonesome Glee' and Poetics of Emptiness", highlights work of an American poet Emily Dickinson's part of a long meditative tradition, and investigates how her poetics of emptiness is marked by a negative tendency that resonates with Daoism and Chan Buddhism. Topics discussed include Dickinson's poetics of emptiness derives from an image cluster that has the air and wind as a basis, and linking with her efforts to celebrate meditation. ②

Glenn Hughes, in "Love, Terror, and Transcendence in Emily Dickinson's Poetry", argues that the profound appreciation of transcendence by poet Emily Dickinson that guides her lifelong spiritual quest. Topics covered include the experiences of mental pain and torture in her poems, the spiritual explorations detailed in her poetry manifest a struggle and strong aversion to many core tenets of the Christian religion, and her religious life and personality which is expressed in her poetry. ③

---

① Nashar C. "Their Conceptual Dickinson: Emily Dickinson in the Work of Tan Lin and a. j. carruthers". Women's Studies, 2018, 47(3):263-285.

② Kang Y. "Dickinson's Air/Wind: 'Lonesome Glee' and Poetics of Emptiness". Renascence, 2018, 70(4):273-295.

③ Hughes G. "Love, Terror, and Transcendence in Emily Dickinson's Poetry". Renascence, 2014, 66(4):283-304.

## 5. New Criticism

Mustafa Zeki Cirakli, in "The Language of Paradox in the Ironic Poetry of Emily Dickinson", argues that Emily Dickinson's poetry is characterized by her emphasis on ironic use of discourse that amounts to her persistent manifestation of individuality against hypocrisy and vanity. She exerts her peculiar poetic language in a way that helps deplore as well as explore the paradoxical human condition. This paper argues that Dickinson produces a language of poetry, which, in Cleanth Brooks' terms, provides the reader with the "language of paradox". Dickinson's ironic poetry exemplifies Brooks' idea that ironic poetry is self-conscious and satiric in nature and is made up of a language of paradox. The study, therefore, aims to reveal how the language of paradox in Dickinson's poetry yields to irony which is primarily associated with her salient assertiveness, isolation and strong individuality. [①]

## 6. Psychoanalytical Criticism

Peter Boxall, in "Blind Seeing: Deathwriting from Dickinson to the Contemporary", traces a tradition of what is here called "deathwriting" as it stretches from Emily Dickinson, to Franz Kafka, to Samuel Beckett, to Cormac McCarthy. The work of all these writers, the essay argues, is driven by the urge to give a poetic form to the experience of death, to make death thinkable and narratable. Alongside this tradition of deathwriting, and interwoven with it, one can

---

① Cirakli M Z. "The Language of Paradox in the Ironic Poetry of Emily Dickinson". Journal of History, Culture and Art Research. 2015, 4(2):24-38.

discern too, a fascination with "blind seeing", an attempt to make darkness visible, or to overcome the distinction between the light and the dark, the visible and the invisible. In reading the connection between deathwriting and blind seeing as it runs from Dickinson to the contemporary, the essay argues that these writers allow us to glimpse a differently constituted relationship between the living and the dead, and between the perceptible and the imperceptible. At a contemporary moment when it has become urgent to rethink our apparatuses for world picturing, with the emergence of the Anthropocene as a critical context for all of our imaginings, the essay offers this history of deathwriting as a radically different way of seeing, without the aid of human light.[①]

Simon du Plock, in "Emily Dickinson: Metaphorical Spaces and the Divided Self", argues that the life and work of the mid-19th century poet Emily Dickinson has attracted considerable attention in recent years from literary critics, biographers, and contemporary poets on both sides of the Atlantic. Simon suggests a number of possible reasons for renewed interest in this reclusive, intensive writer. He makes a case (with reference to her seminal work) for her particular significance to modern psychology, and especially to my own discipline of existential-phenomenological therapy. He also argues that her unique contribution is grounded in her attempts, via what may be thought of as "a philosophical and philological probing", to chart the metaphorical architecture of the brain, and to describe the experience of being a "divided self"—of fragmentation or splitting of the mind.[②]

Carol J. Cook, in "Emily Dickinson: Poet as Pastoral Theologian", argues that—mystic, rebel, recluse, genius, skeptic, poet, pastoral theologian? Who was Emily Dickinson? Among other descriptors, Dickinson (1830-1886) was a complex

---

① Boxall P. "Blind Seeing: Deathwriting from Dickinson to the Contemporary". New Formations, 2017(89/90):192-211.

② Du Plock S. "Emily Dickinson: Metaphorical Spaces and the Divided Self". Existential Analysis, 2013, 24(2):268-280.

19th century woman who possessed great intellectual and poetic gifts, whose life and work retains tantalizing mysteries, and who can be considered a fascinating "woman out of order" in her time and still in ours (Stevenson-Moessner & Snorton). Immersing oneself in the stories that continue to spin around her life and ongoing discussion about the meaning of her poems can be a rewarding, inspiring adventure, and in what follows, Carol attempts to show how at least some of her poems can be considered artistic expressions of pastoral theology. [1]

Seth Archer, in "*I Had a Terror*: Emily Dickinson's Demon", examines what it calls the mental illness of poet Emily Dickinson through her poetry and through Seth's own experience of a similar condition. Dickinson's poem *I Had a Terror* is interpreted as referring to a panic attack. Seth describes his own panic attack and points out that because of modern psychopharmacology he is able to live a normal life. Without the medication, he says, he would have to live a life of seclusion similar to Dickinson's. [2]

Linda Freedman, in "And with What Body Do They Come?": Dickinson's Resurrection", presents how poet Emily Dickinson's sense of theology and poetry shared common ground, but it does not pretend to declare a truce between religion and literature, reference to her several poems and the sense of irrecoverable loss which is carried by Dickinson's sensitivity to mourning and bereavement in her poetry. [3]

---

[1] Cook C J. "Emily Dickinson: Poet as Pastoral Theologian". Pastoral Psychology, 2011, 60(3): 421-435.

[2] Archer S. "*I Had a Terror*: Emily Dickinson's Demon". Southwest Review, 2009, 94(2):255-273.

[3] Freedman L. "'And with What Body Do They Come?': Dickinson's Resurrection". Religion & Literature, 2014, 46(1):180-187.

## 7. Narratology Study

William Logan, in "Dickinson's Nerves", examines American poet Emily Dickinson's writing style. Topics include the use of "I" to start numerous poems, reversals, the dramatics of meter, rhythm, metaphors, and syntax. Also analyzed are the differences in the rules of engagement of various languages, punctuation, and several of Dickinson's poems. These poems include *The Winter's Tale* and *I felt a Funeral*.[①]

## 8. Thematic Study

Patsy J. Daniels, in "The Gap in Emily Dickinson's Consciousness: Buddhism in Emily Dickinson's Poetry", argues that Emily Dickinson's poetry is associated with Buddhist thought in many ways. A connection may be made between her seclusion and eastern practices. Seclusion offered the opportunity for her to explore her mind. She describes her inner life in her poetry, and her descriptions sound much like descriptions of meditative states. The Transcendentalists influenced her, and her poetry is also associated with Buddhist thought in many other ways. Thus, the Transcendentalists looked east for their inspiration, and she looked even further. Her inner life is reflected in her poems, as descriptions of meditative states.[②]

---

① Logan W. "Dickinson's Nerves". Hudson Review, 2017, 69(4):541-577.
② Daniels P J. "The Gap in Emily Dickinson's Consciousness: Buddhism in Emily Dickinson's Poetry". Jackson State University Researcher, 2007/2008, 21(3):1-31.

# Chapter 12

# Edgar Allan Poe

Edgar Allan Poe excelled in several types of writing, publishing tales of terror and supernatural agency, detective stories, romantic and narrative poetry, burlesques, hoaxes, and literary criticism. As a magazine editor, he hoped to elevate American literature to world prominence; he therefore rejected the idea that there should be a specifically national character to American writing, and severely criticized contemporary authors when they failed to meet his standards. Quarrelsome, temperamental, alcoholic, unreliable, he made few friends and many enemies. The facts of his life, the most melodramatic of any of the major American writers of his generation, have been hard to judge, but lurid legends about him circulated even before he died, some of which were spread by Poe himself.

Poe always put his highest stock in poetry, which he called a "passion" and not merely a "purpose". As he remarked in *The Philosophy of Composition*, poetry, even more than fiction, provides the possibility of taking the reader out of body, in effect out of time, through "that intense and pure elevation of soul" which can come with "the contemplation of the beautiful". In a life filled with a tangled mess, the pursuit of the beautiful in works of art motivated Poe's writing to the very end.

## Critical Perspectives

### 1. Aesthetic Study

Erin E. Forbes, in "Edgar Allan Poe and the Great Dismal Swamp: Reading Race and Environment after the Aesthetic Turn", offers criticism of the poem *Dream-Land* by Edgar Allan Poe. It explores the characteristics of the poem in terms of environment and race following its aesthetic turn. It discusses the claims of the poem in transcending into everyday life, and the aesthetics in the American literary history. [1]

Daniel Hoffman, in "Edgar Allan Poe: The Artist of the Beautiful", discusses the life and poetry of American author Edgar Allan Poe; childhood; tragedies which marked his life; Poe's first volume of poems, *Tamerlane*; criticism and interpretation of his poems; Poe's influence on poets and authors that succeeded him. [2]

### 2. Canonization Study

Robert Albrecht, in "Song of the Poet: Lost in Translation or Re-discovered in a New Form?", discusses a compact disc (CD) entitled Song of the Poet, which

---

[1] Forbes E E. "Edgar Allan Poe and the Great Dismal Swamp: Reading Race and Environment after the Aesthetic Turn". Modern Philology, 2016, 114(2):359-387.

[2] Hoffman D. "Edgar Allan Poe: The Artist of the Beautiful". American Poetry Review, 1995, 24(6):11-18.

sets various poems to music. Robert outlines the process of turning poems from written form to music to electronic media and discusses copyright issues. He explores the challenges of translating between languages and between media. Particular focus is given to his interpretation of the poems *Annabel Lee* by Edgar Allan Poe, *Mending Wall* by Robert Frost, and *I Hear America Singing* by Walt Whitman. [1]

## 3. Psychoanalytical Criticism

John Samuel Tieman, in "Sergeant Major Edgar Allan Poe", uses psychoanalytic theory to frame Edgar Allan Poe's history as an enlisted man in the United States Army. For Poe, these were years of accomplishments as both artist and soldier. When researching this article, two forms of comment are readily detected. Military historians immediately understand the significance in Poe's meteoric rise to sergeant major. But these writers tend not to appreciate the literary history. Literary historians often note that Poe was an enlisted soldier, but, beyond that, seem not to appreciate that information. In none of this is there any sense that Poe sought, and for two years found, a degree of emotional stability. The social structure of the army contained and maintained Poe's psychic structure. This intertwining of the military and the literary, coupled with an understanding of psycho-social development, is the frame needed to understand Sergeant Major Poe. [2]

---

[1] Albrecht R. "'Song of the Poet': Lost in Translation or Re-discovered in a New Form?". ETC: A Review of General Semantics. 2010, 67(2):177-190.

[2] Tieman J S. "Sergeant Major Edgar Allan Poe". International Journal of Applied Psychoanalytic Studies, 2016, 13(4):351-366.

## 4. New Historicism

Philip D. Beidler, in "Mythopoetic Justice: Democracy and the Death of Edgar Allan Poe", focuses on the mystery involved in the strange death of the poet Edgar Allan Poe. To update the cultural connection, Poe, it also turns out, could easily have explained to me why, as recently as 20 years ago, in my hometown of Tuscaloosa, Alabama, it was illegal to sell beer, wine, or liquor on election day. Nor would the historic interest of the conversation have been diminished by the fact that the town in question, the seat of the state university and the state hospital for the insane, had also once, in its days as the old frontier capital, flourished as one of the literary epicenters of "Southwestern Humor", including service as the fictional site of some the most celebrated episodes in the career of the rapscallionish hero of Johnson Jones Hooper's 1845 *Adventures of Captain Simon Suggs*, itself a roistering, vicious parody of Jacksonian campaign biography. It was the final playing out of a political theater of the absurd that Edgar Poe would have understood. It may have been the final act of the political drama that he saw in his last moments on earth. [1]

## 5. Cultural Study

Christopher Peterson, in "Possessed by Poe: Reading Poe in an Age of Intellectual Guilt", enters the debate over the French appropriation of Poe not by seeking redress for the supposed political misdeeds of either Poe or the French, but

---

[1] Beidler P D. "Mythopoetic Justice: Democracy and the Death of Edgar Allan Poe". Midwest Quarterly, 2005, 46(3):252-267.

rather, by addressing itself to the American response to the French reception of Poe. While American cultural studies critics in particular have sought to hold the French accountable for ignoring Poe's troubling biography—one in which the question of Poe's relationship to, and possible support of, antebellum slavery remains unanswered to this day—Christopher argues that the important question of how we as critics situate ourselves in relation to material history is too often buried under a moralizing rhetoric of accountability. Following from, and extending, Jacques Derrida's notion of "spectrality", Christopher maintains that material history is itself a kind of conjuration that belies any strict distinction between the material and the immaterial. Against the demand for accountability, the notion of history-as-conjuration allows us to address questions of historical responsibility in a manner that circumvents the impulse to hold Poe accountable for his crimes.①

---

① Peterson C. "Possessed by Poe: Reading Poe in an Age of Intellectual Guilt". Cultural Values, 2001, 5(2):198-220.

# Chapter 13

# Ezra Pound

Ezra Pound was born in Hariley, Idaho. Although his view of poetry would seem to exclude the long poem as a workable form, Pound could not overcome the traditional belief that a really great poem had to be long. He hoped to write such a poem himself, a poem for his time, which would unite biography and history by presenting his mind and memory. To this end he began working on his cantos in 1915. The cantos were separate poems of varying lengths, combining reminiscence, meditation, description, and transcriptions from books Pound was reading, all of which were to be forged into unity by heat of the poet's imagination. Looking for an explanation of what had gone wrong, Pound came upon the "social credit" theories of Major Clifford Hugh Douglas, a social economist who attributed all the ills of civilization to the interposition of money between human exchanges of goods. At this point, poetry and politics fused in Pound's work, and he began to search for a society in which art was protected from money and to record this search in poems and essays. This became a dominant theme in his cantos.

## Critical Perspectives

## 1. New Historicism

Christos Hadjiyiannis, in "We Need to Talk About Ezra: Ezra Pound's Fascist Propaganda, 1935-1945", argues that Ezra Pound's Fascist Propaganda, 1935-1945 calls attention to the extensive propaganda work that Ezra Pound undertook (both paid and gratis) in the years before and during World War II on behalf of the British Union of Fascists, Mussolini's Fascist Italy, and the short-lived Nazi satellite Said Republic. Feldman presents compelling evidence that challenges the view that Pound was an "accidental" or "aloof" fascist, and that exposes him as a dedicated and fervent fascist propagandist. While Feldmans thesis that Pound was a devout believer in the "political religion" of fascism fails to capture the complexity of his thought and activism at the time, it sheds light on this dark—and curiously understudied—aspect of Pound's career, significantly adding to our knowledge of Pound's fascist work. Primarily for this reason, it is an invaluable contribution to Pound scholarship, and one that deserves a wide readership, even if it lacks the finesse, scope, and depth of more scholarly accounts of Pound's work. [1]

---

[1] Hadjiyiannis C. "We Need to Talk About Ezra: Ezra Pound's Fascist Propaganda, 1935-1945". Journal of Modern Literature, 2015, 39(1):112-126.

## 2. Cultural Studies

Tanja Klankert, in "Strange Relations: Cultural Translation of Noh Theatre in Ezra Pound's Dance Poems and W. B. Yeats's *At the Hawk's Well*", draws on the reception of Noh drama by Ezra Pound and William Butler Yeats, analyses both the literary and cultural "translations" of this form of Japanese theatre in their works, focusing on Yeats's play *At the Hawk's Well* (1917). Tanja conceptualizes "cultural translation" as the staging of relations that mark a residual cultural difference. Referred to as "foreignizing" in translation theory, this method enables what Erika Fischer-Lichte has termed a "liminal experience" for the audience—an effect Yeats intended for the performance of his play. It evokes situations in which opposites collapse and new ways of acting or new combinations of symbols can be tried out. Yeats's play is used to sketch how an analysis of relations could serve as a general model for the study of cultural transfer as cultural translation in general".①

Diego Pellecchia, in "Ezra Pound and the Politics of Noh Film", suggests that poet Ezra Pound's engagement in disseminating Noh overseas was crucially stimulated by the vision of Noh films in the late 1930s. Topics discussed include the turning point in Pound's engagement with Noh, the reason that Pound appreciated the didactic propaganda film, and the period of intense didactic production for Pound in the 1930s.②

Qingjun Li, in "Ezra Pound's Poetic Mirror and the 'China Cantos': The

---

① Klankert T. "Strange Relations: Cultural Translation of Noh Theatre in Ezra Pound's Dance Poems and W. B. Yeats's *At the Hawk's Well*". Word & Text: A Journal of Literary Studies & Linguistics, 2014, 4(2):98-111.

② Pellecchia D. "Ezra Pound and the Politics of Noh Film". Philological Quarterly, 2013, 92 (4):499-516.

Healing of the West", argues that of all non-Asian figures in twentieth-century American literature, Ezra Pound (1885-1972) had the most overt relation to China. Pound made Confucianism an integral part of his project of rethinking the future of the West and committed himself to updating Confucian values to correspond to social changes in the modern world. In this article, Qingjun analyzes Pound's Canto XIII and Cantos LIII, LV, and LVI from the "China Cantos", arguing that Pound used poetry as his medium to mirror those Confucian values that he felt were indispensable for the healing of Western civilization and culture. Pound's use of Chinese characters and concepts in his "China Cantos" therefore acts as an intaglio, mirroring onto the reader the truth that Pound believed: whenever Confucian ideas were put into action, the human experience was the better for it; and if the West could appropriate these ideals and values, its decay could be healed.①

Ce Rosenow, in "'High Civilization': The Role of Noh Drama in Ezra Pound's *Cantos*", offers criticism on the epic poem *Cantos* by American author Ezra Pound. Ce focuses on the importance of Noh drama in Pound's poetry, suggesting that Pound viewed Noh as a representation of civilization and art in Japan and used it in the poem to counterbalance his views of the destruction of civilization. Ce also explores references to Noh in *Cantos*, including Canto IV and *The Pisan Cantos*.②

## 3. Biographical Study

Charles Lock, in "Ezra Pound in Athens: Words Spoken to Zissimos

---

① Li Q. "Ezra Pound's Poetic Mirror and the 'China Cantos': The Healing of the West". Southeast Review of Asian Studies, 2008, 30:41-54.

② Rosenow C. "'High Civilization': The Role of Noh Drama in Ezra Pound's *Cantos*". Papers on Language & Literature, 2012, 48(3):227-244.

Lorenzatos in 1965", argues that there is some confusion evident in biographies concerning Ezra Pound's movements at the time of his eightieth birthday, on 30 October 1965. A little-known source from Greece establishes the dates of the week that Pound and Olga Rudge spent in Athens, and fills in some of the details as to whom he met and which sites he was shown. The recollections of Zissimos Lorenzatos (1915-2004) are themselves not always accurate, nor entirely without their own purposes, especially with regard to the role played by George Seferis. Sorting the chronology, the essay considers what it might have meant for Pound to visit Greece for the first time; Lorenzatos's memories are used to assess the weight of the words spoken by Pound in Greece, words that resonate in Canto CXVI.[①]

## 4. Psychoanalytical Criticism

Ian Freckelton, in "Fitness to Stand Trial: Learning from the Ezra Pound Saga", argues that the famous United States poet and literary figure Ezra Pound (1885-1972) was indicted for treason in the District of Columbia after being extradited from Italy for participation during the Second World War in propaganda broadcasts on behalf of the Italian dictator, Benito Mussolini. With his life at risk, he successfully pleaded that he was unfit to stand trial by reason of mental impairment. A review of the evidence given by the four psychiatrists and of the judge's charge to the jury casts doubt on the claim that the trial was politically directed to ensure that Pound was not executed. However, later diagnoses from St. Elizabeths Hospital in Washington, after he was detained, suggest that his principal impairment may have been a personality disorder, perhaps with cyclothymic or bipolar traits, raising the issue of whether such a diagnosis should be sufficient for a

---

① Lock C. "Ezra Pound in Athens: Words Spoken to Zissimos Lorenzatos in 1965". Journal of Modern Literature, 2015, 39(1):72-86.

finding of unfitness to stand trial.[1]

## 5. Comparative Study

Robert Zamsky, in "Ezra Pound and Charles Bernstein: Opera, Poetics, and the Fate of Humanism", offers a comparison of Ezra Pound's *Le Testament* and Charles Bernstein's *Shadowtime*. A brief background on how Pound and Bernstein turned to opera is given. The allegorical elements of both works, their choice of main characters and the idea of humanism reflected in these works, are discussed. The influence of text-setting in the development of an opera and the function of music in pedagogy per Plato's teachings are also tackled.[2]

Reed Way Dasenbrock, in " 'Paradiso ma non troppo': The Place of the Lyric Dante in the Late Cantos of Ezra Pound", analyzes the influence of poet Dante on the poem *The Cantos*, by Ezra Pound; difference between the works of Dante and Pound; reason behind the difficulty in distinguishing the relevance of the non-epic work of Dante in the epic work of Pound; background on the works of Dante.[3]

## 6. New Historicism

Andrea Rinaldi, in "Caged verses: Some New Notes on the Politics of *The Pisan Cantos*", argues that *The Pisan Cantos* is the most notorious section of Pound's masterpiece *The Cantos*, which was named after the concentration camp of

---

[1] Freckelton I. "Fitness to Stand Trial: Learning from the Ezra Pound Saga". Psychiatry, Psychology & Law, 2014, 21(5):625-644.

[2] Zamsky R. "Ezra Pound and Charles Bernstein: Opera, Poetics, and the Fate of Humanism". Texas Studies in Literature & Language, 2013, 55(1):100-124.

[3] Dasenbrock R W. " 'Paradiso ma non troppo': The Place of the Lyric Dante in the Late Cantos of Ezra Pound". Comparative Literature,2005, 57(1):45-60.

Coltano, near Pisa, where Pound was imprisoned by the US army after the fall of Italian Fascism. There, the exiled American poet was detained in the infamous "gorilla cage" because of his propagandist activity in favour of Mussolini and his regime, for which he was indicted for treason against his own homeland. Despite his inhuman treatment, Pound wrote there some of the most renowned and appreciated verses of the twentieth century, worthy of the first Bollingen Prize as awarded to him in 1949 by the Fellows in American Letters of the Library of Congress. Apart from their undisputable artistic value, praised for decades by critics, these verses also attained an important political function, inspiring generations of fascist intellectuals and activists. This article aims to shed further light on this political relevance by uncovering archival material not yet analysed by scholars. [1]

Barry Ahearn, in "Ezra Pound and Otto Kahn", argues that Ezra Pound's obsessive concern with economics and the role of the Jews began in 1932. Yet there is no consensus about the immediate cause of this fateful turn. A look at the relation between Pound and Otto Kahn, however, indicates that Pound's unhappiness with Kahn must have been a contributing factor. Their relation was at its most intense in 1931 and 1932. During those years, Pound appealed to Kahn to come to the aid of such writers as Louis Zukofsky and George Oppen. Kahn politely deflected these appeals. Pound's failure to move Kahn convinced him that capitalism could not provide a living wage for the true artist, either in the "free market", or in the form of funds from a wealthy patron. Therefore, a radical reconstruction of economics was necessary. After 1932, Pound considered Kahn symptomatic of economic injustice and (eventually) racial degeneration. [2]

Jon Schneider, in "Ezra Pound: Foreign Correspondent", focuses on the

---

[1] Rinaldi A. "Caged Verses: Some New Notes on the Politics of *The Pisan Cantos*". Vegueta: Anuario de la Facultad de Geografía e Historia, 2019(19):381-401.

[2] Ahearn B. "Ezra Pound and Otto Kahn". Journal of Modern Literature, 2009,32(2):118-132.

contributions of poet and journalist Ezra Pound to the Virginia newspaper *Richmond News Leader*. It mentions an editorial article "Keynes Brainwashed Electorate with Economic Hogwash" written by Pound which was published by the newspaper on July 14, 1959. The essay represents the first and last publication of Pound for the Virginia newspaper. Pound's writings for the paper remained unprinted and unknown which were kept by his editor, James J. Kilpatrick. His link with the newspaper dates back to 1941 when he started recording his notorious broadcasts for Radio Rome's "The American Hour" wherein he attacked and made slanderous criticisms against politicians and other persons or institutions. [1]

Chantal Bizzini, in "The Utopian City in *The Cantos* of Ezra Pound", focuses on the process of city building discussed in the book *The Cantos*, by Ezra Pound. Overview of the various stages of development of a historical city; information on real cities where Pound actually lived, including Venice, Italy; emergence of a utopian city from the images of real and mythical cities. [2]

Massimo Bacigalupo, in "America in Ezra Pound's Posthumous Cantos", presents information on the writings of Ezra Pound. "Canti postumi" presents material written by Pound over fifty years, from the *Three Cantos* of 1917 in the Poetry text, to some "Lines for Olga" that he composed not long before his death in homage to his loyal companion. Therefore, as one reviewer suggested, Canti postumi is a sort of Cantos in a nutshell, since we are confronted with Pound's various ways of writing, from the more discursive style of circa 1915, to the visionary allusiveness of the 1920s, to the toughening of the 1930s to the breaking down and recovery of the 1940s, to the "atomic" style of the 1950s and the final

---

[1] Schneider J. "Ezra Pound: Foreign Correspondent". Virginia Quarterly Review, 2008, 84(2): 218-237.

[2] Bizzini C. "The Utopian City in *The Cantos* of Ezra Pound". Utopian Studies, 2004, 15(1):30-43.

softening as "Old Ez" approaches death.①

## 7. Aesthetic Study

David Barnes, in "Fascist Aesthetics: Ezra Pound's Cultural Negotiations in 1930s Italy", argues that although the nature of Ezra Pound's Fascism has generated substantial critical study, the mechanics of his actual engagement in the cultural projects of the Mussolini regime has received less attention. Using as its starting point lines from Pound's controversial "Italian Canto" 72—explicit in its praise of the Fascist regime—the essay examines Pound's correspondence with Italian cultural figures in the 1930s. Focusing on his relationship with the academic librarian Manlio Torquato Dazzi and the celebrated Futurist F. T. Marinetti, the essay demonstrates the blurred distinctions between aesthetic and political spheres in Pound's engagements with Italian culture in the 1930s. The essay further argues that Pound's avant-garde aesthetics and neo-platonic philosophy colored the way he engaged with the cultural projects of the regime, making his Fascism a mixture of spirituality, modernism and totalitarianism.②

## 8. Translation Study

Kimberly Fairbrother Canton, in "Opera as Translation: Ezra Pound's *Le Testament*", argues that in Ezra Pound's *Le Testament*, the first of his three operatic compositions, the relentless drive for linguistic precision is undermined by

---

① Bacigalupo M. "America in Ezra Pound's Posthumous Cantos". Journal of Modern Literature, 2003, 27(1/2):90-98.

② Barnes D. "Fascist Aesthetics: Ezra Pound's Cultural Negotiations in 1930s Italy". Journal of Modern Literature, 2010, 34(1):19-35.

an ironic recourse to the imprecise, even mystical, signifying capacity of music and rhythm. Given Pound's lifelong engagement with translation, it is likely not surprising that his turn to opera was essentially literary in purpose, serving the poet as a means to "translate" the category of poetic language he termed melopoeia (in this case, François Villon's *Le Testament*). What is surprising, however— particularly given Pound's notorious fascist sympathies and his own esoteric poetic style—is Pound's determination to make this poetry accessible, intellectually and materially. Though *Le Testament* unapologetically valorizes Villon's poems for their unique difficulty, the use of opera (and later radio opera) as the means of translation reflects Pound's desire to make Villon's poetry "sing" to the masses— calling into question the common conflation of modernist difficulty with modernist elitism. [1]

## 9. Canonization Study

Rachel Blau Duplessis, in "Elliott Carter's Ezra Pound", discusses the musical compositions of American composer Elliott Carter that were based on the poems of poet Ezra Pound, particularly the *On Conversing with Paradise*. The work, which was premiered by the Birmingham Contemporary Music Group on June 20, 2009, was based on Pound's *The Pisan Cantos*". [2]

---

[1] Canton K F. "Opera as Translation: Ezra Pound's *Le Testament*". University of Toronto Quarterly, 2010, 79(3):941-957.
[2] Duplessis R B. "Elliott Carter's Ezra Pound". Chicago Review, 2014, 58(3/4):173-186.

# Chapter 14

# Henry Wadsworth Longfellow

Henry Wadsworth Longfellow was born in Portland, Maine (then still a part of Massachusetts), the second of eight children. Both of his parents encouraged his early interest in reading and writing. Longfellow was the most beloved American poet of the nineteenth century. As literary modernism took hold in the twentieth century, Longfellow came to be seen as an unadventurous, timid poet, but such an assessment unfairly diminishes the achievement of a writer who saw value in working with (rather than against) established forms and traditions. Viewed in relation to his own culture and his own poetic aspirations, Longfellow exhibited a metrical complexity, a mastery of sound and atmosphere, a progressive social conscience, and a melancholy outlook that belied his persona as a soothing white-bearded fireside poet. In his own time, Longfellow was as popular for the challenges he posed to his reading public as for his poetic reassurances.

## Critical Perspectives

### 1. Cultural Study

John Morton, in "Longfellow, Tennyson, and Transatlantic Celebrity", explores the celebrity culture and lion-hunting associated with Alfred Tennyson and Henry Wadsworth Longfellow, argues that while both poets experienced enormous literary fame during their lifetimes, the celebrity culture surrounding them might have been a motivating factor in their subsequent decline in popularity, and the Modernist depreciation of nineteenth-century poetry. Exploring the ways in which Longfellow courted celebrity culture, the article turns to the lion-hunting exploits of Edward Bok, a Dutch-American magazine editor, to demonstrate the desire of Longfellow's readers to physically encounter him. Examining the intense media coverage attending Longfellow's travels to Britain in 1868-1869, the article underlines his status as the ultimate American literary celebrity of the period, but also positions Longfellow as a "lion-hunter" by focusing on his meeting with Tennyson on the Isle of Wight in 1868, and on the way in which their encounters in person and in print reveal contrasting attitudes to celebrity. [1]

Andrew C. Higgins, in "Evangeline's Mission: Anti-Catholicism, Nativism, and Unitarianism in Longfellow's *Evangeline*", argues that though *Evangeline* has long been considered simply a love story, this article reads the poem as one deeply involved in both the theological and cultural struggles between the Catholic and

---

[1] Morton J. "Longfellow, Tennyson, and Transatlantic Celebrity". Critical Survey, 2015, 27(3): 6-23.

Protestant churches in the antebellum period. The essay argues that Longfellow's poem about the Acadian Expulsion of 1755 imagines those Catholic refugees as successful immigrants to America. Further, the article argues that Longfellow's vision of Philadelphia at the end of the poem is that of an ideal, ecumenical Christian community, in which Catholicism is able to coexist with various Protestant churches. Thus the poem counters anti-Catholic nativist rhetoric that portrayed Catholics as fundamentally foreign and a threat to the Republic. However, the ecumenical nature of this vision is limited by the fact that Longfellow cannot imagine a fully-realized Catholic Church in the United States; his Catholic community lacks ecclesiastical hierarchy. As such, it reflects Longfellow's connection to the Unitarian Moralists, as group of Harvard Unitarians who sought to transform other denominations rather than to convert individuals to Unitarianism. [1]

## 2. Canonization Study

Lloyd Willis, in "Henry Wadsworth Longfellow, United States National Literature, and the Canonical Erasure of Material Nature", discusses the views of authors and literary critics George Santayana and Van Wyck Brooks on the works and literary manifestos of poet Henry Wadsworth Longfellow and the impact of Longfellow's removal from the U. S. literary canon on the U. S. literature. Longfellow had envisioned an environmentally determined national literature. He believed that any national literature would have to base its claims of vitality and originality on the qualities of its natural environment. For Santayana and Brooks, Longfellow's literary manifestos were unimportant and his vision of trans-Atlantic

---

[1] Higgins A C. "Evangeline's Mission: Anti-Catholicism, Nativism, and Unitarianism in Longfellow's *Evangeline*". Religion & the Arts, 2009, 13(4):547-568.

literary unity seemed weak-minded and unimaginative.[1]

Nicholas A. Basbanes, in "Famous Once Again", looks at poet Henry Wadsworth Longfellow. According to Dana Gioia, chairman of the National Endowment for the Arts, Longfellow did as much as any author or politician of his time to shape the way 19th-century Americans saw themselves, their nation, and their past. To commemorate Longfellow's 200th birthday during February 2007 the U.S. Postal Service has issued a commemorative stamp. A Library of America edition of his selected writings, published in 2000, has gone through four printings. The article discusses Longfellow's wife Fanny Appleton, his published works, including *Evangeline*, and his popularity.[2]

Joseph C. Murphy, in "Ántonia and Hiawatha: Spectacles of the Nation", presents on the childhood recital of Willa Cather of the poem *Song of Hiawatha* by Henry Wadsworth Longfellow. Topics include the impact of Longfellow on Cather, Cather's enthusiasm for Longfellow which prompted her to absorbed Longfellow's verse in some of her characters and Cather's novel *My Ántonia* which is conceived as a template for Americanization and American identity.[3]

## 3. New Historicism

Agnieszka Salska, in "From National to Supranational Conception of Literature: the Case of Henry Wadsworth Longfellow", discusses the life and works of author and poet Henry Wadsworth Longfellow and traces the evolution of his poetic program away from the assertive nationalism of his youth to the firm

---

[1] Willis L. "Henry Wadsworth Longfellow, United States National Literature, and the Canonical Erasure of Material Nature". ATQ, 2006, 20(4):629-646.
[2] Basbanes N A. "Famous Once Again". Smithsonian, 2007, 37(11):96-103.
[3] Murphy J C. "Ántonia and Hiawatha: Spectacles of the Nation". Cather Studies 2017, 11:64-90.

universalism of his late years. Longfellow withdrew in the 1860s from the immediate cultural concerns in the U. S. to commune with the supranational ideal of art. He paid little attention to his national mission in the poems he published during and following the Civil War. His late works emphasize the inner life of the artist, his uneasy relation to the world and his struggle against time and oblivion. He also moved from the folk-inspired ballad and narrative tale to the more exclusive poetic drama. [1]

Mark Niemeyer, in "Henry Wadsworth Longfellow's *Evangeline*: *A Tale of Acadie* and the Ambiguous Afterlife of the History of the Acadians", argues that Longfellow's *Evangeline* was hailed as a great and distinctively American work when it appeared in 1847, and the poem's use of North American history was a key element in its favourable reception. This use of history, however, is ambiguous and complex. The epic continues, first of all, in a long tradition of romanticized retellings of the heart-rending story of the Acadians. But the work also engages in a dual-level dialogue with both the mid-eighteenth-century history of the Acadians, who are pitied, without inciting indignation, and the contemporary history of mid-nineteenth-century America, whose expansionism it both implicitly celebrates and criticizes. [2]

David Haven Blake, in "Among the English Worthies: Longfellow and the Campaign for Poets' Corner", argues that in 1884, a bust of Henry Wadsworth Longfellow was unveiled in Poets' Corner, Westminster Abbey, positioning the American between memorials to Geoffrey Chaucer and John Dryden. Longfellow was the first foreign author thus honoured, and his selection created transatlantic controversy. Through newspapers and correspondence, this article explores how

---

[1] Salska A. "From National to Supranational Conception of Literature: the Case of Henry Wadsworth Longfellow". ATQ, 2006, 20(4):611-628.

[2] Niemeyer M. "Henry Wadsworth Longfellow's *Evangeline*: *A Tale of Acadie* and the Ambiguous Afterlife of the History of the Acadians". Canadian Review of American Studies, 2018, 48(2):121-145.

Longfellow's bust came to be in Poets' Corner, tracing the role of its organizer, Dr. William Cox Bennett, his benefactors in government and the Palace, and a host of distinguished contributors to the campaign. While nineteenth-century celebrity is often described as a public phenomenon accompanied by crowds of cheering admirers, the memorialization campaign centred on transatlantic elites who praised Longfellow's virtue, humility, and internationalism. The article examines how the campaign shaped the meaning of both Poets' Corner and late nineteenth-century transatlantic fraternity and argues that it also became the setting for conflicting ideas about literature, cosmopolitanism, national memory, and Victorian racial theories.①

Stephen Harrigan, in "House of Fatherly Dreams", discusses the historic home of 19th-century U. S. author Henry Wadsworth Longfellow located in Cambridge, Massachusetts. Stephen explains how the home was once used as the headquarters of U. S. General and future President George Washington for a period during the American Revolution. He notes his experience taking a tour of the house. Also discussed is the death of Longfellow's wife, Fanny Appleton Longfellow, in the house due to a fire, Longfellow's depressive nature, and his various travels throughout Europe. Focus is given to the design of the house's study.②

Jill Lepore, in "How Longfellow Woke the Dead", argues that when first published 150 years ago, his famous poem about Paul Revere was read as a bold statement of his opposition to slavery. The contemporary reception of the poem *Paul Revere's Ride*, by Henry Wadsworth Longfellow, first published in the January 1861 issue of *The Atlantic Monthly*. It considers the lifelong friendship between Longfellow and eventual senator and abolitionist Charles Sumner, who met in 1837

---

① Blake D H. "Among the English Worthies: Longfellow and the Campaign for Poets' Corner". Critical Survey, 2015, 27(3):82-104.

② Harrigan S. "House of Fatherly Dreams". American History, 2013, 48(2):54-61.

when both men where teaching at Harvard University and maintained an active correspondence when separated. Also considered are Longfellow's reactions to events such as the Fugitive Slave Act, the U. S. Supreme Court's Dredd Scott decision, and John Brown's raid on Harpers Ferry, Virginia. ①

## 4. Comparative Study

Angus Fletcher, in "Whitman and Longfellow: Two Types of the American Poet", compares the styles of the poetry of Henry Wadsworth Longfellow and Walt Whitman; historical position in American literary esteem; Whitman's art of syntactic manipulation; Longfellow's art of poetic reciprocation; establishment of art of liminal poetics. ②

---

① Lepore J. "How Longfellow Woke the Dead". American Scholar, 2011, 80(2):33-46.
② Fletcher A. "Whitman and Longfellow: Two Types of the American Poet". Raritan, 1991, 10(4):131.

# Chapter 15

# Walt Whitman

Walt Whitman revolutionized American poetry. Responding to Emerson's call in *The Poet* (1842) for an American bard who would address all "the facts of the animal economy, sex, nutriment, gestation, birth," he put the living, breathing, sexual body at the center of much of his poetry, challenging conventions of the day. Responding also to Emerson's call for a "metre-making argument" rather than mere meters, he rejected traditions of poetic scansion and elevated diction, improvising the form that has come to be known as free verse, while adopting a wide-ranging vocabulary opening new possibilities for poetic expression. A Poet of democracy, Whitman celebrated the mystical, divine potential of the individual; a poet of the urban, he wrote about the sights, sounds, and energy of the modern metropolis. In his 1855 preface to *Leaves of Grass*, he declared that "the proof of a poet is that his country absorbs him as affectionately as he has absorbed it".

## Critical Perspectives

### 1. New Historicism

Mark Edmundson, in "Walt Whitman's Guide to a Thriving Democracy", examines the contributions of 19th-century American poet Walt Whitman to the U.S. national identity and democracy. Topics covered include Whitman's relationship with poet Ralph Waldo Emerson, Whitman's work of poetry *Song of Myself*, and Whitman's religious beliefs. [1]

Vanessa Steinroetter, in "Walt Whitman in the Early Kansas Press", talks about American poet, essayist, and journalist Walt Whitman dealing with the history of the press in Kansas and his views on the American democracy. Topics include his association with former President Abraham Lincoln, literary works on U.S. politics and national identity, and his role in the Weekly Kansas Chief founded by Solomon Miller. [2]

Timothy Robbins, in "Emma Goldman Reading Walt Whitman: Aesthetics, Agitation, and the Anarchist Ideal", focuses on the aesthetics, agitation and anarchist ideal of the literary works of Walt Whitman. It mentions that the literary works of Whitman embodies antiwar and the incarnation of the country's anarchist menace. It adds that the political readings of Whitman's work signifies the division

---

[1] Edmundson M. "Walt Whitman's Guide to a Thriving Democracy". Atlantic, 2019, 323(4): 100-110.
[2] Steinroetter V. "Walt Whitman in the Early Kansas Press". Kansas History, 2016, 39(3): 182-193.

between the political life of the country and literary art.①

Scott Holland, in "*The Poet*, Theopoetics, and Theopolitics", explores the influence of the theopoetics of philosopher Ralph Waldo Emerson on poet Walt Whitman and Transcendentalist author Moncure Daniel Conway. It reflects on the radicalism of Whitman and the religious aspects of the book *Leaves of Grass* which explore the themes of body and soul. Other topics include the task of self-creation, abolitionism, and the essay *Circles*.②

Ryan J. Davidson, in "Transatlantic Intersections: The Role of Ralph Waldo Emerson in the Dissemination of Blakean Thought into the Poetry of Walt Whitman", argues that Whitman quoted no one in his poetry, at least not directly, as Matt Miller convincingly argues in Collage of Myself. However, Whitman was not above making use of the work of other writers in his poetry. It is through Whitman's early reading in conjunction with his collage approach to composition that he came to create *Leaves of Grass* as something which appears wholly original, but which resonates with so many echoes. It is often argued that Ralph Waldo Emerson is one of the most important influences on Whitman's *Leaves of Grass*. The extent and significance of Emerson's influence has been a subject of inquiry since the advent of Whitman scholarship. This text will focus on Emerson's essays and lectures as the main influences on Whitman which can be read as providing a mediating influence between Blake and Whitman.③

Ed Folsom and Jerome Loving, in "The Walt Whitman Controversy: A Lost Document", discusses the relationship between American authors Mark Twain and

---

① Robbins T. "Emma Goldman Reading Walt Whitman: Aesthetics, Agitation, and the Anarchist Ideal". Texas Studies in Literature & Language, 2015, 57(1):80-105.

② Holland S. "*The Poet*, Theopoetics, and Theopolitics". Cross Currents, 2014, 64(4):496-508.

③ Davidson R J. "Transatlantic Intersections: The Role of Ralph Waldo Emerson in the Dissemination of Blakean Thought into the Poetry of Walt Whitman". Hawliyat, 2016(17):33-50.

Walt Whitman. Although people think that Whitman's *Leaves of Grass* and Twain's novels share certain characteristics, it was only during the last years of Whitman that he was occasionally referred to Twain. As a writer, Whitman once said that Twain mainly misses fire. As for his personal relationship with Twain, Whitman regarded him as friendly, but not warm. Twain confronted the hypocrisy surrounding authors by writing the article "The Walt Whitman Controversy" in 1882. But, apart from the controversy, what lingers in that hovering final fragment is Twain's affirmation of the nobility of Whitman's work, something he never affirmed quite so directly anywhere else.[1]

## 2. Canonization Study

Philippa Tudor, in "Holst, Vaughan Williams and Walt Whitman", reflects on American poet Walt Whitman and his poem *Leaves of Grass* which inspired several English composers including Charles Wood and Charles Villiers Stanford. Topics discussed include composer Ralph Vaughan Williams's musical piece "Sea Symphony", poems selected by Wood from Whitman's *Drum Taps* book collection, a table showing composer Gustav von Holst and Vaughan Williams's Whitman compositions, and orchestral works composed by Holst.[2]

## 3. Psychoanalytical Criticism

David Shaddock, in "A Universe Between My Hat and Boots: Whitman's Self

---

[1] Folsom E, Loving J. "The Walt Whitman Controversy: A Lost Document". Virginia Quarterly Review, 2007, 83(2):122-127.

[2] Tudor P. "Holst, Vaughan Williams and Walt Whitman." Musical Times, 2018, 159(1945):3-26.

as a Model for Empathic Connection", argues that the Poems of the great American poet Walt Whitman are herein considered as a guide to psychoanalytic treatment. Whitman's expanded sense of self is described and compared to other, modern and postmodern views. The exquisite intimacy Whitman shows to everything in the world is compared to contemporary relational perspectives. Whitman's empathy, in which he becomes the people he is describing, is viewed as a model for psychotherapy. His view of the body as the seat of the soul is compared to contemporary views of "embodied psychoanalysis". Whitman's view of trauma and loss, especially as it pertained to the Civil War, is described. A case vignette of a couple in which a Whitmanesque view of an expanded view of each partners' self guided the therapist's response concludes the paper.[1]

Abdullah Kurraz, in "Revisiting Walt Whitman's *Song of Myself*: The Poetics of Human Self and Identity", explores the constituents of Walt Whitman's poetic self-soul and body; its hopes, tensions, expectations and concerns. It focuses mainly on *Song of Myself* for it presents a web of references and implications to the poet's fragmented self and confused identity. Whitman portrays his self as such in its human and universal context, expecting other selves to identify with his. In its psychoanalytic ground, the paper also tries to shed light on the poetic anticipation that foreshadows the current hard situations that cause a lot of shocks, fragmentation, depression, uncertainty, and disappointment. According to Whitman's poetics, the absence of stable selves, the loss of hopes and the confusion on place and time provide a ground for exploring human desires and hopes of having stable selves and integrated and identified identities. This paper also studies the fusion between the self and identity as seen in the identification of the

---

[1] Shaddock D. "A Universe Between My Hat and Boots: Whitman's Self as a Model for Empathic Connection". Psychoanalysis: Self & Context, 2019, 14(3):323-333.

poet's self with other people's selves, in search for uniqueness, stability, and social and psychological mobility. ①

## 4. Philosophical Study

Luke Philip Plotica, in "Singing Oneself or Living Deliberately", argues that the individual stands at the center of the works of Walt Whitman and Henry David Thoreau. Prompted to their reflections by the changing social, economic, and political conditions of nineteenth century America, they articulate two rich and distinct visions of individuality and the conditions that foster and frustrate its development. Whitman's poetry and prose depicts a porous, malleable, internally plural self who experiences the world in largely aesthetic terms and ecstatic terms, whereas Thoreau's writings depict a bounded, willful self who experiences the world through the mediating force of her individual ethical principles. Thus, while both valorized individuality they present competing ideals: Whitman's was expansive and centrifugal while Thoreau's was integral and centripetal. Furthermore, their respective accounts of democracy—the former's laudatory, the latter's critical—are profoundly shaped by these antecedent accounts of the individual. In this essay Luke argues that not only do these distinct visions of individuality continue to speak to us today, they stand to inform analysis of and attachment to modern democratic institutions and practices. ②

---

① Kurraz A. "Revisiting Walt Whitman's *Song of Myself*: The Poetics of Human Self and Identity". An-Najah University Journal for Research, B: Humanities, 2015, 29(8):1577-1596.

② Plotica L P. "Singing Oneself or Living Deliberately". Transactions of the Charles S. Peirce Society, 2017, 53(4):601-621.

## 5. Comparative Study

As mentioned in Chapter 4, Ryan J Davidson, in "A Proposal for Revaluation: Points of Contact and Sides of Likeness between William Blake and Walt Whitman", proposes an approach to evaluate the relationship between William Blake and Walt Whitman.

# Chapter 16

# Robert Frost

Robert Frost was born in California and lived there until his father died, when Frost was eleven. The clarity of Frost's diction the colloquial rhythms, the simplicity of his images, and above all the folksy speaker—these are intended to make the poems look natural, unplanned. In the context of the modernist movement, however, they can be seen as a thoughtful reply to high modernism's fondness for obscurity and difficulty. Although Frost's ruralism affirmed the modernist distaste for cities, he was writing the kind of traditional, accessible poetry that modernists argued could no longer be written. In addition, by investing in the New England terrain, he rejected modernist internationalism and revitalized the tradition of New England regionalism.

Frost achieved an internal dynamic in his poems by playing the rhythms of ordinary speech against formal patterns of line and verse and containing them within traditional forms. The interaction of colloquial diction with blank verse is especially central to his dramatic monologues. To Frost traditional forms were the essence of poetry, material with which poets responded to flux and disorder (what, adopting scientific terminology, he called "decay") by forging something permanent. Poetry, he wrote, was "one step backward taken", resisting time—a "momentary stay against confusion".

## Critical Perspectives

### 1. Thematic Study

Joel Westerdale, in "Fiat homo: Redeeming Frost via Nietzsche", states that Robert Frost demonstrated that his most famous poem is best read as an exemplar of Nietzschean amor fati. Topics discussed include his poem *The Road Not Taken* focusing on individualism and the hearty pioneer spirit; poem *Orange is the New Black* on racism; and his poem depicting American culture. [1]

Peter J. Stanlis, in "Robert Frost and Darwin's Theory of Evolution", discusses Robert Frost's acquired interest in Charles Darwin's theory of evolution and analyzes the assumed conflict in doctrines and perspectives between science and religion. What Frost meant by rethinking his belief in God and the claims of the revolutionary theory by Darwin; Frost's open-mindedness regarding Darwin's theory; Frost's dualistic and metaphorical approach to evolution. [2]

### 2. New Historicism

Roger Mills, in "The President and the Poet", recalls former U.S. President John F. Kennedy's Robert Frost, where our nation's leader saluted the arts and

---

[1] Westerdale J. "Fiat homo: Redeeming Frost via Nietzsche". Massachusetts Review, 2018, 59(2):281-288.
[2] Stanlis P J. "Robert Frost and Darwin's Theory of Evolution". Modern Age, 2000, 42(2): 145.

pledged to support them. Topics discussed include Kennedy's speech at the convocation at Amherst College gymnasium; political structure of the U. S. and his motivation, and direction towards the politics.①

Robert Stilling, in "Between Friends: Rediscovering the War Thoughts of Robert Frost", reflects on the poem *War Thoughts at Home* by Robert Frost exemplifies the stories of two friends in Frost's life. The first was Edward Thomas, who died during the World War I. The second story depicts the friendship of Frost with Frederic G. Melcher, a rising star in the book trade. The poem deals in that moment before darkness, doubting the necessity of the bravery that drives a soldier-poet like Thomas to enlist. Its doubt stands at odds with the poet's own stoic convictions about war and violence. Meanwhile, issues of fragmentation and disconnection that haunt the last stanza of the poem are addressed.②

## 3. Ethical Study

Jeff Frank, in "Love and Ruin(s): Robert Frost on Moral Repair", argues that where Alasdair MacIntyre's *After Virtue* begins: facing a moral world in ruin. MacIntyre argues that this predicament leaves us with a choice: we can follow the path of Friedrich Nietzsche, accepting this moral destruction and attempting to create lives in a rootless, uncertain world, or the path of Aristotle, working to reclaim a world in which close-knit communities sustain human practices that make it possible for us to flourish. Jeff Frank rejects MacIntyre's framework and in this essay attempts to create an alternative path, one of moral repair. Through a close reading of several poems from Robert Frost's North of Boston, Frank develops the

---

① Mills R. "The President and the Poet". Massachusetts Review, 2018, 59(2):271-280.
② Stilling R. "Between Friends: Rediscovering the War Thoughts of Robert Frost". Virginia Quarterly Review, 2006, 82(4):113-119.

notion of moral repair and describes its ethical and educational implications. ①

## 4. Comparative Study

Paula Kopacz, in "Claiming Place: Robert Frost and Jesse Stuart", argues that Robert Frost and Jesse Stuart are both known as regional artists. In fact, Frost's use of his New England region was pointed out to Stuart as a model by a literary mentor at Vanderbilt shortly after the publication of the Southern Agrarian manifesto *I'll Take My Stand*. Indeed, there are many similarities between the two men: both were farmers and nature writers, teachers and educators, and above all, regional writers who captured the flora and fauna and character of their respective regions. Despite their different regions, both men take an honest and authentic look at the unsettling and sometimes cruel ironies of nature and the human condition: the appearance of rustic simplicity that the Yankee and the Appalachian artist tease us into taking at face value nevertheless provokes the Truth of deep probing into the meaning of life. As successful regional artists, Appalachian Stuart and New England Frost claim their place not only in geography, but more importantly, in American literary tradition as each one uses his intimate knowledge of place and character to spin a wonderfully entertaining read, whether it be in prose or verse. Most similar when they are linked by the jarring effect of final lines (Frost) and the ironic disjunction between content and title (Stuart), both writers ultimately, often surprisingly, strike the reader with the hard edge of universal truth about what it means to be human. ②

John Edgar Tidwell, in "Two Writers Sharing: Sterling A. Brown, Robert

---

① Frank J. "Love and Ruin(s): Robert Frost on Moral Repair". Educational Theory, 2011, 61 (5):587-600.

② Kopacz P. "Claiming Place: Robert Frost and Jesse Stuart". Journal of Appalachian Studies, 2011, 17(1/2):177-187.

Frost, and *In Dives' Dive*", argues that literary influence can be a reciprocating theme of sharing through an analysis of the poets Sterling A. Brown and Robert Frost. John discusses the influence and intertextuality of these two American poets, exploring the significance of the poem *In Dives' Dive*, by Frost on the work of Brown. He also examines their overlapping views of literary history and analyzes how both men sought to find their place in society by portraying politics in their works of poetry.[①]

## 5. Cultural Study

R. Clifton Spargo, in "Robert Frost and the Allure of Consensus", discusses the poetry of author Robert Frost and responds to the common idea that his popularity connotes a lack of complexity and seriousness. R. Clifton sees Frost's work as reflecting awareness of the patterns of everyday speech. Frost's use of the commonplace, or cliché, is seen as a way of experimenting with the language, examining the motives of the speaker and showing awareness of the historical concepts behind the language. He also sees Frost's playing with cliché as a manifestation of a democratic culture, which accepts shared history and reinterprets it for the current time. He believes that Frost was fascinated by the dynamic tension between questioning tradition and the need for obedience, community, and acknowledgment of shared circumstances.[②]

Dan Diephouse, in "The Economic Impulse in Robert Frost", examines the extent to which personal material economic circumstances and the cultural economic ethos for poetry writing affected Robert Frost. It looks into how some of Frost's

---

[①] Tidwell J E. "Two Writers Sharing: Sterling A. Brown, Robert Frost, and *In Dives Dive*'". African American Review, 1997, 31(3):399-408.

[②] Spargo R C. "Robert Frost and the Allure of Consensus". Raritan, 2009, 28(3):38-65.

poetry was informed by these circumstances. The article also examines how and to what degree the poet sublimated the material issue into an aesthetic. Frost's best poems, *Birches* and *After Apple-Picking*, reflect the different concepts of economics and aesthetics, vocation and avocation, work and life, home economy and natural economy. His poems reflect the way he sees work in human and communal terms. [1]

## 6. Thematic Study

Sherman J. Clark, in "Frost for Lawyers: *The Best Thing That We're Put Here For's to See*", discusses the book *The Poetry of Robert Frost: The Collected Poems* edited by Edward Connery Lathem, focusing on an analysis of why lawyers should read the literary works created by Frost. Work-life balance and lawyering in America are mentioned, along with Frost's poems *A Passing Glimpse* and *The Tuft of Flowers*. Pragmatism and a reported tension between life and law are examined, as well as issues such as aspiration and self-delusion. [2]

Thomas Duddy, in "The Sadness that Lurks: Robert Frost and the Poetry of Poverty", on *Poetry and Poverty*, states that in his address Frost expressed his sympathy towards poor people and admitted that he understands the plight of poor through his own experiences. Thomas informs that throughout his life Frost has experienced financial insecurities and has been involved into variety of jobs like farmer and teacher. [3]

---

[1] Diephouse D. "The Economic Impulse in Robert Frost". Criticism, 2006, 48(4):477-507.
[2] Clark S J. "Frost for Lawyers: *The Best Thing That We're Put Here For's to See*". Michigan Law Review, 2014, 112(6):867-882.
[3] Duddy T. "The Sadness that Lurks: Robert Frost and the Poetry of Poverty". Hudson Review, 2011, 64(3):445-461.

## 7. Psychoanalytical Criticism

Lisa Hinrichsen, in "A Defensive Eye: Anxiety, Fear and Form in the Poetry of Robert Frost", argues that Robert Frost's poems enact a poetic and psychic process of displacing and managing generalized anxiety through converting it into object-specific fear. Drawing upon the psychoanalytical work of Sigmund Freud, Dominick LaCapra and Eric Santner, this essay analyzes how and why Robert Frost's poems display a "defensive eye": a self-protective relationship to the world dependent upon a continual switching of visual and linguistic perspectives that diffuses the pressures interior to the poem and creates a "momentary stay against confusion". Through close readings of *The Vantage Point*, *The Mending Wall*, *The Wood-Pile*, *The Fear*, *An Old Man's Winter Night* and *A Considerable Speck*, the essay traces Frost's visual preoccupation with boundaries, walls, doors, and frames that demarcate spatial limits, and describes how the poem negotiates the psychological and linguistic tension between containment and catharsis.[①]

Keat Murray, in "Robert Frost's Portrait of a Modern Mind: The Archetypal Resonance of *Acquainted with the Night*", interprets the poem *Acquainted With the Night*, by Robert Frost, which focuses on the concept of the persona; observations by psychologists Carl Jung and Joseph Campbell; use of poetic form and language; persona's conception of the night; symbolism of the persona's venture in the darkness, water and light; word choice and rhythm.[②]

---

[①] Hinrichsen L. "A Defensive Eye: Anxiety, Fear and Form in the Poetry of Robert Frost". *Journal of Modern Literature*, 2008, 31(3):44-57.

[②] Murray K. "Robert Frost's Portrait of a Modern Mind: The Archetypal Resonance of *Acquainted with the Night*". *Midwest Quarterly*, 2000, 41(4):370.

## 8. New Criticism

Naser Emdad and Md. Ariful Islam Laskar, in "Design, Darkness and Duality: Defamiliarization in Frost's Poetry", argues that Robert Frost, a true representative of American literature, deals with the idyllic pastoral landscape of America and traces the transition of American life and society of his time in a lucid way. He is highly rated and esteemed as a pastoral poet. Though the diction of his poems apparently seems to be simple, many of these poems deal with complex and philosophical themes. Sometimes, the level of complexity is so high that the readers become intrigued and deceived and it instigates the readers' thoughts to a great extent. Frost intentionally brings odd and weird imageries and symbols or "something sinister" which works as a pattern or design for Frost's poetry and this process defamiliarizes his poems and presents them as a new wine in an old bottle. In the core of many of Frost's poems we find that there dwells a macabre, eccentric, and lonely feature of human life wearing the terrifying "design of darkness" in the lap of a gentle, meek, and picturesque nature. In essence, this paper is an effort to find out and show how Frost focuses on the design of darkness and duality, and deeply penetrates nature to acquaint his readers with a deeper meaning of life and its surroundings in a sing-song and pleasant voice by skillfully applying the technique of defamiliarization. [1]

---

[1] Emdad N, Laskar M A I. "Design, Darkness and Duality: Defamiliarization in Frost's Poetry". ASA University Review, 2013, 7(1):37-44.

# Chapter 17
# T. S. Eliot

The publication in 1922 of *The Waste Land* in the British little magazine *Criterion* and the *American Dial* was a cultural and literary event. The poem's title and the view it incorporated of modern civilization seemed, to many, to catch precisely the state of culture and society after World War I. The war, supposedly fought to save European civilization, had been the most brutal and destructive in Western history: what kind of civilization, after all, could have allowed it to take place? The long, fragmented structure of *The Waste Land*, too, contained so many technical innovations that ideas of what poetry was and how it worked seemed fundamentally changed. A generation of poets either imitated or resisted it. The author of this poem was an American living in London, T. S. Eliot, he had a comfortable upbringing in St. Louis: his mother was involved in cultural and charitable activities and wrote poetry, his father was a successful businessman.

## Critical Perspectives

### 1. New Historicism

Steven Matthews, in "Literary and Political Hinterland of T. S. Eliot's *Coriolan*", argues that there has been an increased amount of scholarly interest lately in T. S. Eliot's unfinished sequence, *Coriolan* (1932)—interest drawn from its Shakespearian allusiveness, and from analysis of this writings particularly rebarbative, jarring poetic. Although, however, the two parts of the sequence published by Eliot are acknowledged as being his nearest approach to poetic commentary upon contemporary political ideas, little criticism exists establishing the hinterland of the political thought, with which Eliot was most familiar, as editor of the Criterion. *Coriolan* emerges at a time when the lure of fascism pulled hardest at Eliot's sensibility. This article reviews the full political context provided by Eliot's journal, as well as considering the connections between that political engagement and the readings of Shakespeare he was also promulgating through this forum, in order to provide a more complex sense than hitherto of the diverse pressures underlying the unsettled nature of the existing *Coriolan* poems. [1]

Michael Simpson, in "Oedipus, Suez, and Hungary: T. S. Eliot's Tradition and *The Elder Statesman*", discusses *The Elder Statesman*, a play by T. S. Eliot that put in an isolated appearance in 2008 as a rehearsed reading at the King's Head, Islington, where it was performed by the theater group Primavera as part of

---

[1] Matthews S. "Literary and Political Hinterland of T. S. Eliot's *Coriolan*". Journal of Modern Literature, 2013, 36(2):44-60.

its "Forgotten Classics" series. It notes that John Osborne's *Look Back in Anger* had opened in London, England, leading to a revolution in British theater that probably obscured the success of Eliot's drama. It proposes a conjunction between *The Elder Statesman* and *Look Back in Anger*. ①

## 2. Canonization Study

Andrey Astvatsaturov, in "On the Way towards Canon-formation: The Case of T. S. Eliot", presents an attempt to highlight the historical and cultural background of formation of Eliot's canon, as well as to analyze certain aesthetic paradigms that formed its basis (the theory of tradition, the conception of impersonal poetry, and the concept of "dissociation of sensibility"). In the article, the key figures belonging to the canon are mentioned, and the reasons for their canonization are identified. Particular attention is paid to Eliot's take on the problem of dialogue of cultures, and of acquisition of a foreign poetical tradition, as well as to the principles that, according to Eliot, should govern literary translation. ②

## 3. Philosophical Study

Edward Upton, in "Language in the Middle Way: T. S. Eliot's Engagement with Madhyamaka Buddhism in *Four Quartets*", traces the influence that Buddhist texts had on the poetic design and philosophical orientation of T. S. Eliot's *Four Quartets*. References to the "middle way" in the poems point us to texts from the

---

① Simpson M. "Oedipus, Suez, and Hungary: T. S. Eliot's Tradition and *The Elder Statesman*". Comparative Drama, 2010-2011, 44/45(4/1):509-528.

② Astvatsaturov A. "On the Way towards Canon-formation: The Case of T. S. Eliot". World Literature Studies, 2019, 11(1):42-50.

very earliest moments of the Buddhist tradition, texts to which Eliot had access. More specifically, Edward develops the suggestion offered by Jeffrey Perl and Andrew Tuck that the work of Nagarjuna, the second-century founder of the Madhyamaka school of Buddhism (the so-called "Middle Way" school), could have played an important role in T. S. Eliot's philosophical and poetic development. Edward employs Perl and Tuck's assertion as a hermeneutical lens through which to analyze Eliot's work and suggests that Eliot's allusions to the "middle way" in *Four Quartets* can usefully be understood through Nagarjuna's causal analysis and linguistic theories, themselves codifications in part of the earlier Buddhist priorities. [1]

Muhammad Saleem, Akhtar Ali and Shazia Kousar, in "*The Waste Land* by T. S. Eliot: A Site for Inertia in Motion", analyzes T. S. Eliot's poem *The Waste Land* with reference to the theme of stasis in the apparently mobile life of the twentieth century Europe. The poetic sensibility of Eliot aestheticises the barrenness of the modern life in the backdrop of spiritual bankruptcy. The horizontal motion is measured with the yardstick of paradigmatic axis. Boredom, monotony and meaninglessness are the various manifestations of stillness in the spiritually barren modern world. The poet makes use of different artistic devices to foreground his concerns on this modern dilemma. Self-critical text, suggestive alternative point of view, use of grand-narrative in the modern context, inter-textual references, contrastive modes of description and metaphoric images are some of them. This study is pursued in the light of these poetic strategies to draw upon the stopped up life of the current Europe. The variety of mechanical activities of the age makes face at the theoretical framework of the modern existence. [2]

---

[1] Upton E. "Language in the Middle Way: T. S. Eliot's Engagement with Madhyamaka Buddhism in *Four Quartets*". Journal of the American Academy of Religion, 2018, 86(3):821-850.
[2] Saleem M, Ali A, Kousar S. "*The Waste Land* by T. S. Eliot: A Site for Inertia in Motion". Gomal University Journal of Research, 2015, 31(2):182-193.

Francesca Bugliani Knox, in "Between Fire and Fire: T. S. Eliot's *The Waste Land*", presents on the intellectual interest in religious mysticism of poet T. S. Eliot and his poem *The Waste Land*. Topics discussed include mystical Christian tradition popularized by author Evelyn Underhill which is the thread that connect themes and details of poems, Eliot's acknowledgment of the philosophy of philosopher Rudolph Eucken regarding religious expression, and author Jessie Weston who suggested Eliot the plan of the poem *The Waste Land*.[①]

Jūrate Levina, in "Speaking the Unnameable: A Phenomenology of Sense in T. S. Eliot's *Four Quartets*", argues that through its ostensibly philosophical rhetoric and multiple allusions, *Four Quartets* manifests a continuity between T. S. Eliot's poetic thought and his early engagement with philosophy. The thematic core of this continuity is Eliot's concern with the meaningful experience of reality, described as equally dependent on direct perception and on linguistic structure. language shapes perception into a meaningful world-vision, while experience itself is an ongoing process of interpreting (or signifying) that which is perceived. This link empowers poetic language, entangling the reading consciousness in a process to which Edmund Husserl's descriptions of consciousness refer as "sense-giving". *Four Quartets* epitomizes both the phenomenological description and the poetic enactment of meaningful experience. Its opening movement both mimics the structure of experienced reality and keeps the reading eye in the process of making sense in its full complexity, involving all faculties of apprehending reality, from the metaphysical logo-centric systems underlying conceptual understanding of the world to the direct sensuous perception of immediate environment.[②]

---

① Knox F B. "Between Fire and Fire: T. S. Eliot's *The Waste Land*". The Heythrop Journal, 2015, 56(2):235-248.

② Levina J. "Speaking the Unnameable: A Phenomenology of Sense in T. S. Eliot's *Four Quartets*". Journal of Modern Literature, 2013, 36(3):194-211.

## 4. Cultural Study

Alastair Morrison, in "Beyond Bad Faith: Cultural Criticism and Instrumentality", argues for the role of instrumental thinking in cultural and literary criticism, practices sometimes thought of as naturally anti-instrumental. Focusing on the work of Matthew Arnold and T. S. Eliot, it shows a shared instrumental defense of Christianity but also how, for situational reasons, this defense has made instrumentalism harder to locate within the Anglophone critical tradition. Arnold promoted adherence to the national church on openly civic and functional grounds, though to do so he had to derogate the idea, widely held by British Christians, that the metaphysical truth of Christianity outweighed practical considerations. Eliot, in a career of apologetics that consciously emended Arnold's, offered a similarly effectual sense of Christianity's value but enfolded this valuation into a model of cultural holism that forbade individual acts of if/then calculation, avoiding the appearance of bad faith. Eliot's holism becomes part of Raymond Williams's conception of the agency of the cultural despite Williams's lack of interest in the specifically religious project. In brief, the rhetorical difficulty of instrumentalizing Christianity drives instrumental calculation underground, making it illegible against the larger backdrop of romantic anti-utilitarianism in cultural politics. This essay suggests that, when the object is not belief, instrumental approaches to culture present fewer contradictions than is often assumed and that it may be an opportune moment to reconsider them.[①]

Hazel Atkins, in "Raising *The Rock*: The Importance of T. S. Eliot's Pageant-Play", examines the development of British poet T. S. Eliot's concept of

---

① Morrison A. "Beyond Bad Faith: Cultural Criticism and Instrumentality". Criticism, 2019, 61 (2):167-189.

community, tradition, and ritualism in art in his play *The Rock*. It offers a background of Eliot's reason for writing the play which centers on the building of a church. Hazel infers that critics of *The Rock* have overlooked the fact that despite its flaws, the pageant-play typifies Eliot's transformation into a Christian writer and his special interest in rituals and church symbolisms. ①

Anthony Domestico, in "The Twice-Broken World: Karl Barth, T. S. Eliot, and the Poetics of Christian Revelation", presents on the relation between poet T. S. Eliot and theologian Karl Barth. It compares Barth's *Epistle to the Romans* to Eliot's early poetry, exploring the reaction to historical crises that resulted in a crisis of representation. Also, it compares Eliot's dialectical poetics to the analogical poetics of poet Gerard Manley Hopkins. It examines the sharp contrast between what Eliot's poetry asserts and what it enacts. ②

Alan Blackstock, in "Chesterton, Eliot, and Modernist Heresy", discusses the orthodoxy and heresy by writers G. K. Chesterton and T. S. Eliot. Topics include Chesterton's 1908 book *Orthodoxy*, lectures delivered by Eliot at the University of Virginia in 1933, and the relationship of Eliot to modernism. Particular focus is also given to Chesterton's 1905 book *Heretics*. ③

Martin Warner, in "Reading the Bible 'as the Report of the Word of God': The Case of T. S. Eliot", focuses on the case of Thomas Stearns Eliot, wherein he reads the Bible "as the Report of the Word of God". It says that Eliot's preferred traditional mode of reading, not as fundamentalist, but as authoritative witness to religious truth. It mentions that the biblical resonance of Eliot mature poetry is often

---

① Atkins H. "Raising *The Rock*: The Importance of T. S. Eliot's Pageant-Play". Christianity & Literature, 2013, 62(2):261-282.

② Domestico A. "The Twice-Broken World: Karl Barth, T. S. Eliot, and the Poetics of Christian Revelation". Religion & Literature, 2012, 44(3):1-26.

③ Blackstock A. "Chesterton, Eliot, and Modernist Heresy". Renascence, 2018, 70(3):199-216.

more imagistic than verbal, directing to "God-fearing" poetic approach to the literary dimension of the Bible. ①

Jewel Spears Brooker, in " 'Our First World': T. S. Eliot and The Edenic Imagination", offers the insights regarding the work of T. S. Eliot that was never been read as a whole because some of his work has been withdrew in archives. He says that Eliot's complete prose, the first volume including over twenty unpublished philosophical essays which is important for clarifying intellectual and spiritual roots of his imagination. He adds that Eliot had an edenic imagination, a religious version of dialectical imagination that transcends and contains contradictions. ②

Craig Woelfel, in "T. S. Eliot and Our Beliefs about Belief", presents on the beliefs regarding religion and literature scholarship and the works of T. S. Eliot. It says that the loss of beliefs defines secularization and modernization. It states that literary-biographer A. D. Moody summarizes the turn away of Eliot from philosophy study in 1914 in terms of Anglo-Catholicism. It adds that the early works of Eliot reflect his background in studies of religious experiences including psychology, mysticism, and sociology. ③

Susan E. Colón, in "*This Twittering World*: T. S. Eliot and Acedia", presents the views regarding the prevalence of acedia in T. S. Eliot's literary works. It highlights Eliot's books where the said mortal sin is present including *The Waste Land*, *Murder in the Cathedral* and *Four Quartets*. It denotes the relational concepts between acedia and laziness. It also denotes the criticism on

---

① Warner M. "Reading the Bible 'as the Report of the Word of God': The Case of T. S. Eliot". Christianity & Literature, 2012, 61(4):543-564.

② Brooker J S. "'Our First World': T. S. Eliot and the Edenic Imagination". Religion & Literature, 2012, 44(1):151-159.

③ Woelfel C. "T. S. Eliot and Our Beliefs about Belief". Religion & Literature, 2012, 44(1): 128-136.

Eliot's views about the sin.①

## 5. Aesthetic Study

Ben J. Richardson, in "'A Conversation with Spectres': Russian Ballet and the Politics of Voice in T. S. Eliot", argues that when Sergei Diaghilev's Ballet Russes first emerged on the pre-war London stage, it was greeted as the herald of an artistic revolution. T. S. Eliot—one of the most outspoken, of often ambivalent, commentators on modern dance—paradoxically sought to approach such radical new aesthetic forms through the notion of "tradition". Ballet in particular performs a dual function within his poetic oeuvre: it is emblematic of both the collapse of human community within modernist spaces, yet also simultaneously represents the possibility of reintegration through transnational modes of experience. It exemplifies, for Eliot, the interpenetration of all expression, suggesting "not only the pastness of the past, but... its presence".②

## 6. Gender Study

Brian Clifton, in "Textual Frustration: The Sonnet and Gender Performance in *The Love Song of J. Alfred Prufrock*", discusses of Eliot's *The Love Song of J. Alfred Prufrock* and focuses on alienation and anxiety or the poem's formal elements. However, there seems to be a gap in explaining how these two aspects relate to each other. Throughout the monologue, Prufrock's attempts to assert his

---

① Colón S E. "*This Twittering World*: T. S. Eliot and Acedia". Religion & Literature, 2011, 43(2):69-90.

② Richardson B J. "'A Conversation with Spectres': Russian Ballet and the Politics of Voice in T. S. Eliot". Journal of Modern Literature, 2013, 37(1):158-177.

(idea of) masculinity seem to be related to how the poem uses and frustrates the sonnet form. If the sonnet is understood as an inherently masculine form and if its appearance (fully or partially) within the poem points toward an attempt to fulfill the social constraints of masculinity, then the poem will allow gender and structure to enter in dialogue, which suggests that Prufrock's inability to perform as masculine is related to his inability to both create and manipulate the sonnet structure. [1]

## 7. Ethical Study

James Matthew Wilson, in "The Formal and Moral Challenges of T. S. Eliot's *Murder in the Cathedral*", discusses the plot of the play, the play's challenge for the contemporary readers to reconsider the assumption regarding the nature of morality, and the formal and historical background of the play. [2]

## 8. New Criticism

James Matthew Wilson, in "Ancient Beauty, Modern Verse: Romanticism and Classicism from Plato to T. S. Eliot and the New Formalism", focuses on the argument of contemporary artists and poets about their position on Classicism and Romanticism literature carried on by T. S. Eliot and other modernists early in the twentieth century. Topics discussed include the description of Classicism and Romanticism in the book *The Mirror and the Lamp*, by M. H. Abrams, the

---

[1] Clifton B. "Textual Frustration: The Sonnet and Gender Performance in *The Love Song of J. Alfred Prufrock*". Journal of Modern Literature, 2018, 42(1):65-76.

[2] Wilson J M. "The Formal and Moral Challenges of T. S. Eliot's *Murder in the Cathedral*". Logos: A Journal of Catholic Thought & Culture, 2016, 19(1):167-203.

genealogy of Romanticism and Classicism, and the controversy between Eliot and John Middleton Murry regarding the theory of modernist art.①

Matthew Scully, in "Plasticity at the Violet Hour: Tiresias, *The Waste Land*, and Poetic Form", argues that for Catherine Malabou, plasticity names what gives or receives form, as well as what potentially annihilates form. Malabou does not propose a liberation from the closure of form but a liberation within form itself. In *The Waste Land*, the metamorphic force of Tiresias, who figures a bodily excess at the approximate center of the poem, announces a disordering impulse from within the poem. Critical approaches to *The Waste Land* have often reproduced Eliot's desire for order by repeatedly privileging ordering logics in readings of the poem's form, especially in readings focused on the role of Tiresias. In contrast, by thinking of Tiresias as a plastic figure and as a figure for the plasticity of *The Waste Land*, we can reconceive the form of *The Waste Land* as that which bears witness to the disordering and excessive force excluded and absented from traditional conceptions of the poem's formal organization.②

---

① Wilson J M. "Ancient Beauty, Modern Verse: Romanticism and Classicism from Plato to T. S. Eliot and the New Formalism". Renascence, 2015, 67(1):3-40.

② Scully M. "Plasticity at the Violet Hour: Tiresias, *The Waste Land*, and Poetic Form". Journal of Modern Literature, 2018, 41(3):166-182.

# Chapter 18

# Langston Hughes

Langston Hughes was the most popular and versatile of the many writers connected with the Harlem Renaissance. Along with Zora Neale Hurston, he wanted to capture the dominant oral and improvisatory traditions of black culture in written form. Hughes was born in Joplin, Missouri. In childhood, since his parents were separated, he lived mainly with his maternal grandmother on Lawrence, Kansas.

Within the spectrum of artistic possibilities open to writers of the Harlem Renaissance—drawing on African American rural folk forms on literary traditions and forms that entered the United States from Europe and Great Britain; or on the new cultural forms of blacks in American cities—Hughes chose to focus his work on modern, urban black life. He modeled his stanza forms on the improvisatory rhythms of jazz music and adapted the vocabulary of everyday black speech to poetry. He also acknowledged finding inspiration for his writing in the work of white American poets who preceded him. Like Walt Whitman he heard America singing, and he asserted his right to sing America back; he also learned from Carl Sandburg's earlier attempts to work jazz into poetry. Hughes did not confuse his pride in African American culture with complacency toward the material deprivations of black life in the United States. He was keenly aware that the modernist vogue in the black among white American was potentially exploitative and voyeuristic; he confronted such racial tourists with the misery as well as the jazz of Chicago's South Side. Early and late, Hughes's poems demanded that African Americans be acknowledged as owners of the culture they gave to the United States and as fully enfranchised American citizens.

## Critical Perspectives

### 1. New Historicism

Steven Hoelscher, in "A Lost Work by Langston Hughes", reports on the rediscovery of a lost essay by African American author Langston Hughes. It mentions Hughes's travel through the South in 1927, his experiences seeing the chain gangs and how they inspired his poem *Road Workers*, and includes the essay he wrote on that experience as an introduction to the novel *Georgia Nigger* by John L. Spivak.[1]

Isabel Soto, in "*I Knew that Spain Once Belonged to the Moors*: Langston Hughes, Race, and the Spanish Civil War", responds to Dolan Hubbard's proposal to enhance scholarship on "Hughes and the international stage", addresses race within the context of Hughes's numerous writings inspired by the Spanish Civil War, which he covered as a war correspondent for the Baltimore Afro-American. Through close readings of a number of texts, Isabel argues that the category of race provides a productive and neglected entry into reading the conflict in which the violent supremacist ideology of Spain's colonial Army of Africa, chief instigators of the 1936 uprising, was contested by the opposing ideology of the African American combatants of the Abraham Lincoln Brigade volunteers. Inscribing race at the heart of the Spanish conflict enables us also to recover a key player in the forced transatlantic dispersal and enslavement of African men and women in the early

---

[1] Hoelscher S. "A Lost Work by Langston Hughes". Smithsonian, 2019, 50(4):20-24.

modern period and to enrich Gilroy's hugely influential paradigm by unearthing Spanish participation as well as recognizing Hughes as a vital black Atlanticist. [1]

W. S. Tkweme, in "Blues in Stereo: The Texts of Langston Hughes in Jazz Music", examines the intersection between the literary works of the mid-20th century African American writer Langston Hughes and contemporary Jazz and Blues music of his era. Introductory comments are given noting how Hughes recognized and commented on African American music in his literature. Questions are then raised evaluating the extent to which Hughes's literature has been received and incorporated into the works of Jazz musicians. [2]

Jonathan Scott, in "Advanced, Repressed, and Popular: Langston Hughes during the Cold War", brings to light an important area of Langston Hughes's work as a writer and an intellectual that has been neglected by critics and scholars. In the discipline of American studies, Hughes is known primarily as a "folk poet", yet in his life he produced an enormous body of work that cannot be contained by this limited categorization, in particular the writing he published during the height of the cold war. The general conception of Hughes is that he went into political hiding after 1953, following his appearance before the House Un-American Activities Committee, and, for the rest of his career, steered clear of socialist projects such as the politicization of literature. But a reflection on his writing of the 1950s compels a different conclusion. Specifically, *The First Book of Rhythms*, published in 1954, based on a writing workshop for young people Hughes conducted in Chicago, is the focus of this paper. It embodies the main themes and strategies that unified

---

[1] Soto I. "*I Knew that Spain Once Belonged to the Moors*: Langston Hughes, Race, and the Spanish Civil War". Research in African Literatures, 2014, 45(3):130-146.

[2] Tkweme W S. "Blues in Stereo: The Texts of Langston Hughes in Jazz Music". African American Review, 2008, 42(3/4):503-512.

Hughes's prolific literary output during the cold war. ①

Sonnet Retman, in "Langston Hughes's *Rejuvenation Through Joy*: Passing, Racial Performance, and the Marketplace", presents on the short story *Rejuvenation Through Joy* which is part of the book *The Ways of White Folks* by Langston Hughes. The short story's use of satire to depict the use of race in U. S. capitalistic culture, including in regard to racial passing and the performance of race, is discussed. ②

Glenn Jordan, in "Re-Membering the African-American Past", argues that the Harlem Renaissance of the 1920s was part of the New Negro Movement that swept the USA in the early twentieth century. Through fiction, poetry, essays, music, theatre, sculpture, painting and illustration, participants in this first Black arts movement produced work that was both grounded in modernity and an engagement with African-American history, folk culture and memory. This paper focuses on two Harlem Renaissance artists, the poet and fiction writer Langston Hughes and the illustrator and mural painter Aaron Douglas, who were particularly concerned with matters of history, memory and meaning. Themes such as the African past, slavery, freedom, lynching and migration figure powerfully in their art; and they employed modes of artistic expression that were accessible to a broad audience of African Americans. Glenn explores such works as Hughes's *The Negro Speaks of Rivers*, *The Negro Mother*, *Afro-American Fragment* and *Aunt Sue's Stories* and Douglas's four-part mural *Aspects of Negro Life*. ③

Don James McLaughlin, in "Langston Hughes's *Ethics of Compromise*: a Review of Which Sin to Bear?", argues that David Chinitz's Which Sin to Bear?:

---

① Scott J. "Advanced, Repressed, and Popular: Langston Hughes during the Cold War". College Literature. 2006, 33(2):30-51.

② Retman S. "Langston Hughes's *Rejuvenation Through Joy*: Passing, Racial Performance, and the Marketplace". African American Review, 2012, 45(4):593-602.

③ Jordan G. " Re-Membering the African-American Past". Cultural Studies, 2011, 25(6):848-891.

Authenticity and Compromise in Langston Hughes explores the poet's interest in the concept of racial authenticity, as well as his growing appreciation of "compromise". The book's greatest contribution is the first published analysis of Hughes's executive-session testimony before Joseph McCarthy's Senate Permanent Subcommittee on Investigations. Released in 2003, the testimony offers new insight into the rhetoric Hughes adopted while under interrogation. While Hughes's equivocations on the communist sentiments expressed in his poetry may strike some as a surrender to McCarthy's scare politics, Chinitz argues that the transcript reveals instead a sequence of deliberately crafted, literary-theoretical rejoinders. This reading serves Chinitz's argument that, across his career, Hughes became increasingly committed to theorizing an "ethics of compromise". [1]

Etsuko Taketani, in "*Spies and Spiders*: Langston Hughes and Transpacific Intelligence Dragnets", presents the navigation of poet Langston Hughes and his knowledge about the intelligence dragnets. Topics discussed include the memoir of Hughes relating to his experience of being harassed by Japanese police in his book *I Wonder as I Wander*, the expulsion of Hughes from Japan after being suspected as a Soviet spy, and being interrogated by former U.S. politician Joseph McCarthy and chief counsel Roy Cohn. [2]

## 2. Cultural Study

John Patrick Leary, in "Havana Reads the Harlem Renaissance: Langston Hughes, Nicolás Guillén, and the Dialectics of Transnational American

---

[1] McLaughlin D J. "Langston Hughes's *Ethics of Compromise*: a Review of Which Sin to Bear?". Journal of Modern Literature, 2015, 38(3):181-184.

[2] Taketani E. "*Spies and Spiders*: Langston Hughes and Transpacific Intelligence Dragnets". The Japanese Journal of American Studies, 2014(25):25-48.

Literature", discusses the aspects of transnationalism in American literature and discusses the misinterpretations in translated cultural literature. He focuses on a letter written by Cuban journalist Gustavo Urrutia to American poet Langston Hughes in 1930, regarding a poetry collection *Motivos de son*, (*Son Motifs*) by Cuban poet Nicolás Guillén. He criticizes Urrutia's interpretation in the letter that *The Weary Blues* by Hughes and *Son Motifs* are similar. [1]

## 3. New Criticism

Paul Williams, in "Physics made Simple: the Image of Nuclear Weapons in the Writing of Langston Hughes", draws upon the Simple stories written by Langston Hughes in the post-war period and argues that Hughes repeatedly drew upon nuclear technology as part of a symbolic vocabulary that articulated American racial injustice, both within and outside the United States. For the character Simple, nuclear weapons are white weapons, deployed in defence of white interests, and whose use has been informed by hierarchies of racial difference. However, this technology also provides potent evidence that Hughes juxtaposes against claims of white racial superiority: how can white America continue to assert its racial maturity, while building weapons capable of extinguishing human life from the planet? Ultimately, the character of Simple asserts that non-military nuclear technology can help construct a future beyond race. [2]

---

[1] Leary J P. "Havana Reads the Harlem Renaissance: Langston Hughes, Nicolás Guillén, and the Dialectics of Transnational American Literature". Comparative Literature Studies, 2010, 47(2):133-158.

[2] Williams P. "Physics made Simple: the Image of Nuclear Weapons in the Writing of Langston Hughes". Journal of Transatlantic Studies (Springer Nature), 2008, 6(2):131-141.

## 4. Queer Study

Shane Vogel, in "Closing Time: Langston Hughes and the Queer Poetics of Harlem Nightlife", reflects the opinion on the sexuality of Langston Hughes. It mentions about rumors that Hughes was a gay, fueled by Hughes's knowledge of sexual underworlds and his literary explorations of overt homosexuality, such as his short story *Blessed Assurance*. Shane also talks about the two events that propelled the speculation about Hughes's sexuality: Arnold Rampersad's biography of Hughes and Isaac Julien's film, "Looking for Langston". [1]

## 5. Cultural Study

Bartholomew Brinkman, in "Movies, Modernity, and All that Jazz: Langston Hughes's *Montage of a Dream Deferred*", presents literary criticism for the poem sequence *Montage of a Dream Deferred* by Langston Hughes. Primary focus is given to depictions of jazz music, particularly bebop, as an essentially African American musical form within the sequence as well as Hughes's thoughts on movies. The anti-capitalist nature of the work is explained based on Hughes's critique of exclusionary U.S. mass culture. [2]

---

[1] Vogel S. "Closing Time: Langston Hughes and the Queer Poetics of Harlem Nightlife". Criticism, 2006, 48(3):397-425.

[2] Brinkman B. "Movies, Modernity, and All that Jazz: Langston Hughes's *Montage of a Dream Deferred*". African American Review, 2011, 44(1/2):85-96.

# Chapter 19

# William Carlos Williams

William Carlos Williams was born in 1883 in Rutherord, New Jersey, a town near the city of Paterson. A modernist known for his disagreements with all the other modernist, Williams considered himself as the most underrated poet of his generation. His reputation has risen dramatically since World War II as a younger generation of poets testified to the influence of his work on their idea of what poetry should be. The simplicity of his verse forms, the matter-of-factness of both his subject matter and his means of describing it, seemed to bring poetry into natural relation with everyday life. He is now judged to be among the most important poets writing between the wars. His career continued into the 1960s, taking new directions as he produced, along with shorter lyrics, his epic five-part poem *Paterson*. The social aspect of Williams's poetry rises from its accumulation of detail; he opposed the use of poetry for general statements and abstract critique.

## Critical Perspectives

### 1. New Historicism

Paul R. Cappucci, in "A Libretto in Search of Music: The Strain of Collaborative Creation in William Carlos Williams's *The First President*", argues that throughout the 1930s and beyond, William Carlos Williams labored on a grand opera entitled *The First President* that "would", as he wrote, "galvanize us into a realization of what we are today" (*Many Loves*). He portrays George Washington as a figure who transforms fear and anxiety into the creative leadership necessary to guide an unstable new country. Williams dreamed of Roosevelt attending his opera and thus fusing the past with the present. Such a project reflects Williams's epic ambition to do something of national import. This paper documents Williams's design for the libretto and his collaborative difficulties; it also contextualizes the project amid the numerous Washington celebrations that occurred throughout the 1930s. By examining the libretto in this way, the paper reveals Williams's increasing investment in the project and ultimate identification with a troubled visionary who persistently overcame betrayals in an effort to help America realize its democratic promise.[①]

Daria Pârvu, in "Celebrating Modern America: William Carlos Williams and

---

[①] Cappucci P R. "A Libretto in Search of Music: The Strain of Collaborative Creation in William Carlos Williams's *The First President*". Journal of Modern Literature, 2013, 36(2):80-104.

His Artist-Friend Charles Sheeler", explores the relationship between William Carlos Williams and his artist-friend Charles Sheeeler and it also examines the extent to which Williams found visual sources of inspiration in Sheeler's art. Williams praised Sheeler in several essays dedicated to his artist-friend for his ability to give the local a universal dimension. Williams, too, tried to emphasize the American vernacular by making use of common, ordinary things in his poems. Both Williams and Sheeler believed that the work of art should possess autonomy, it should have a rather objective than subjective character as well as focus on a more impersonal perspective rather than a personal one. Williams also agreed with Sheeler's belief that a work of art resembled a machine which could serve as both model and subject for the painting and the poem. [1]

Milton A. Cohen, in "Stumbling into Crossfire: William Carlos Williams, *Partisan Review* and the Left in the 1930s", argues that though actively involved in leftist causes and committees throughout the 1930s, William Carlos Williams had an almost uncanny knack for getting between warring factions and alienating power centers of the Left, particularly *Partisan Review*. This paper examines three such incidents: two in which PR intentionally humiliated the poet in 1936-1937, and one in which Williams joined, signed petitions, then resigned from several leftist splinter groups battling each other in 1939. Among the reasons considered for these mishaps are: Williams's political naiveté about factionalism and editorial good faith; his skepticism regarding communism; his desire to be published in the leading leftist magazines; and the byzantine political alignments of the late 1930s. Ironically, Williams's own poetry and fiction in the 1930s show a genuine empathy (without cant or cliché) for the working class—a quality that was more talked about

---

[1] Pârvu D. "Celebrating Modern America: William Carlos Williams and His Artist-Friend Charles Sheeler". Revista Transilvania, 2017(11/12):61-67.

than achieved in leftist circles.[①]

Miguel Mota, in "'It looked perfect to my purpose...' William Carlos Williams's contact with the Spanish", discusses the influence of Spanish literature on author William Carlos Williams' literary style. Compromise made by Williams in the conflict between English and American literature using through his Spanish literary heritage; emphasis on the replacement of certain elements of American poetry with Spanish influences; emphasis on the Spanish American audience.[②]

Peter Monacell, in "In the American Grid: Modern Poetry and the Suburbs", focuses on the work of four modern poets who expressed concerns over the suburbanization of natural and agricultural areas. He argues that, amidst the pre-World War II transformation of the countryside, modern poets questioned the viability of the pastoral mode. These poets sought to determine whether new suburban environments could furnish the natural imagery and poetic individuality that this mode entails. He suggests specifically that William Carlos Williams and Wallace Stevens depict their domestic environments as varieties of suburbs. Their poems demonstrate that suburban Americans can locate or imagine pastoral spaces within residential grids. By contrast, the New York modernists Hart Crane and Louis Zukofsky perceived suburbs as insurmountable obstructions to the pastoral mode and poetic individuality. Modern poetry's variety of responses to suburbanization can enrich our views of American poetry and pastoral writing.[③]

---

[①] Cohen M A. "Stumbling into Crossfire: William Carlos Williams, *Partisan Review* and the Left in the 1930s". Journal of Modern Literature, 2009, 32(2):143-158.

[②] Mota M. "'It looked perfect to my purpose...' William Carlos Williams's Contact with the Spanish". Journal of Modern Literature, 1993, 18(4):447.

[③] Monacell P. "In the American Grid: Modern Poetry and the Suburbs". Journal of Modern Literature, 2011, 35(1):122-142.

## 2. Cultural Study

William Boelhower, in "A Place from Which to Speak: The Gift Economy in Williams's Poem *Morning*", presents literary criticism on the central concern of the poem *Morning*, by William Carlos Williams, which addresses an Italian immigrant enclave on the margins of Paterson, New Jersey. Origin of Williams's special interest in Paterson immigrants; cultural gap between the speaker of the poem and the Italians; reference to ashes in the context of the household economy of the immigrants. [1]

Stephen M. Park, in "Mesoamerican Modernism: William Carlos Williams and the Archaeological Imagination", explores the popularity of Mesoamerican cultures in the U.S. in the 1920s and '30s and considers how these cultures were adopted by members of the U.S. avant-garde as a way of distancing themselves from European traditions and linking themselves with thoroughly "American" art forms. This "Mayan Revival" flourished in the 1920s, particularly among architects who built neo-ruins throughout the U.S. After exploring this cultural context, Stephen then turns to the literary fascination with Mesoamerican cultures, seen most dramatically in the Maya-themed issue of Broom magazine, in which William Carlos Williams's *The Destruction of Tenochtitlan* first appeared. In his quest for an "indigenous" American art, Williams frequently echoed the popular culture's fascination with "reviving" native civilizations. However, Williams's vision was a far more pessimistic one, and the archaeological remains of fallen civilizations of the Americas provided a mordant critique of U.S. greed and consumerism in

---

[1] Boelhower W. "A Place from Which to Speak: The Gift Economy in Williams's Poem *Morning*". Paterson Literary Review, 2005(34):36-45.

Williams's own day.①

## 3. Translation Study

Zhaoming Qian, in "William Carlos Williams, David Raphael Wang, and the Dynamic of East/West Collaboration", presents on the collaborative translation project of William Carlos Williams and David Raphael Wang on the poem *The Cassia Tree*. It mentions that the poem imputes the virtual silence and scrutiny of the authors to the subject of China. However, the authors state that the poem is not a translation to the version of Arthur Waley but rather a re-creations in the American idiom, which is dedicated to the poetic career of William Carlos Williams.②

## 4. Anthropological Study

Joshua Schuster, in "William Carlos Williams, *Spring and All*, and the Anthropological Imaginary", examines the contexts of an "anthropological imaginary" that inform a close reading of William Carlos Williams's *Spring and All* (1923). It seeks to expand the associations of modernism and anthropology from the typical conflation of these terms with the poetry of T. S. Eliot and anthropologist James Frazer by linking Williams's interests with Franz Boas, the most established anthropologist in the United States at the time. Williams's focus on the local is similar to Boas's stress on site-specific observation. But Williams's

---

① Park S M. "Mesoamerican Modernism: William Carlos Williams and the Archaeological Imagination". Journal of Modern Literature, 2011, 34(4):21-47.

② Qian Z. "William Carlos Williams, David Raphael Wang, and the Dynamic of East/West Collaboration". Modern Philology, 2010, 108(2):304-321.

local is the result of a pattern of dislocation in modernity, which Williams incorporates in his poems and turns back against the disembodied scientific language of anthropology that cannot record the participant-observer's disruption and desire. ①

## 5. Comparative Study

George Monteiro, in "The Existence of an American Venus: William Carlos Williams versus Henry Adams", discusses the similarities in the novels of American historian Henry Adams and William Carlos Williams. Influence of Adams's *The Education of Henry Adams* on Williams, *White Mule*; reference to Williams's comparison of the birth of his female to that of Venus. ②

Robert Kusch, in "'My Toughest Mentor': William Carlos Williams and Theodore Roethke (1943-1944)", explores the relationship between Theodore Roethke and William Carlos Williams as writer and mentor; examples of Roethke's works; reputation of Williams in the field; impact of the relationship on the career of both poets. ③

## 6. New Criticism

Linda Funkhouser and Daniel C. O'Connell, in "'Measure' in William Carlos Williams's Poetry: Evidence from His Readings", discusses the poetic style in

---

① Schuster J. "William Carlos Williams, *Spring and All*, and the Anthropological Imaginary". Journal of Modern Literature, 2007, 30(3):116-132.

② Monteiro G. "The Existence of an American Venus: William Carlos Williams versus Henry Adams". Journal of Modern Literature, 1996, 20(2):248.

③ Kusch R. "'My Toughest Mentor': William Carlos Williams and Theodore Roethke(1943—1944)". Journal of Modern Literature, 1989, 16(1):161.

William Carlos Williams's poems *The Botticellian Trees* and *The Catholic Bells*; relationship among pausing, phrasing, syntax, image patterns and rhetorical structure in the poems; use of American idiom and rhythm of speech; visual impact and sound effect of the poetry; summation of measurements for both poems. ①

---

① Funkhouser L, O'Connell D. "'Measure' in William Carlos Williams's Poetry: Evidence from His Readings". Journal of Modern Literature, 1985, 12(1):34.

# Chapter 20
# Sylvia Plath

Plath appropriates a centrally American tradition, the heroic ego confronting the sublime, but she brilliantly revises this tradition by turning what the American Transcendentalist Ralph Waldo Emerson called the "great and crescive self" into a heroine instead of a hero. Seizing a mythic power, Plath transmutes the domestic and the ordinary into the hallucinatory, the utterly strange in her poems. Her revision of the romantic ego dramatizes its tendency toward disproportion and excess, and she is fully capable of both using and mocking this heightened sense of self, as she does in her poem *Lady Lazarus*. For all her courting of excess Plath is a remarkably controlled writer; her lucid stanzas, her clear diction, her dazzling alterations of sound display that control. The imaginative intensity of her poems is her own, triumphant creation out of the difficult circumstances of her life.

## Critical Perspectives

### 1. Psychoanalytical Criticism

Justyna Wierzchowska, in "Love, Attachment and Effacement: Romantic Dimensions in Sylvia Plath's Children Poems", examines seventeen children poems by Sylvia Plath written in the years 1960-1963, in relation to the poetics of romantic love. Drawing on motherhood studies, the maternal shift in psychoanalysis, and attachment theory, it reads love as a continuous human disposition, informed by one's attachment history, and realized at different stages of one's life. It specifically refers to Daniel Stern's and Anthony Giddens's largely overlapping concepts of maternal and romantic love to argue that Plath's children poems are significantly infused with a poetics of romantic love. This poetics, however, becomes gradually compromised by a poetics of ambivalence, withdrawal, and self-effacement.[①]

Humaira Aslam, in "The Animus in Sylvia Plath's Poem: *Daddy*", argues that Sylvia Plath gives vent to the frustration she feels at the loss of her father, whom she loved dearly. There is a sudden outburst of harsh words of revenge against him, which is a proof of her animus possessed nature as a Jungian would call it. It looks as if, she wants to do away with the control that the memory of her father has on her

---

[①] Wierzchowska J. "Love, Attachment and Effacement: Romantic Dimensions in Sylvia Plath's Children Poems". International Journal of English Studies, 2018, 18(2):19-33.

mind.①

Cristina Pipoş, in "An Analysis of Intimacy in Sylvia Plath's Poetry", highlights one of the major characteristics of confessional poetry—that of exposure of intimate life and feelings through poetry. The interest in Sylvia Plath's poems is closely linked to that of her personal life, her marriage to Ted Hughes being one of them. Plath's poems are confessional in style, expressing the lack of interest in life and the sole desire to die. Cristina analyzes two of the poems that are an extraordinary example of expressing the most intimate thoughts through poetry, in the paper.②

Isabelle Travis, in "'I Have Always Been Scared of You': Sylvia Plath, Perpetrator Trauma and Threatening Victims", argues that evil does not exist in isolation. For it to occur, one person must commit an act which is experienced by another person. This would suggest two distinct categories of person in relation to evil: perpetrator and victim. Sylvia Plath's poetry has often been interpreted in terms of accusations against the biographical figures in the poet's life or as a denunciation of patriarchal culture. What these readings have in common is that they situate Plath's speakers in the "victim" position. However, the boundaries between victim and perpetrator are frequently blurred. In *Daddy*, Plath's most (in)famous poem the speaker is both second-generation victim and perpetrator. The shame of the relationship to a Nazi perpetrator forms part of the speaker's definition of herself as a victim. In an earlier poem, *The Thin People*, Plath's portrayal of Nazism's victims is not unambiguous: far from feeling sympathy and pity for

---

① Aslam H. "The Animus in Sylvia Plath's Poem: *Daddy*". Putaj Humanities & Social Sciences, 2015, 22(1):215-218.

② Pipoş C. "An Analysis of Intimacy in Sylvia Plath's Poetry". Bulletin of the Transilvania University of Braşov, Series IV: Philology and Cultural Studies, 2013, 6(1):15-18.

concentration camp survivors, her speaker reacts with a mixture of fear and disgust.①

Arielle Greenberg and Becca Klaver, in "Mad Girls' Love Songs: Two Women Poets—a Professor and Graduate Student—Discuss Sylvia Plath, Angst, and the Poetics of Female Adolescence", argues that the legacy of Sylvia Plath's poetry and the received notion of the teenage girl writer wallowing in self-pity are discussed in terms of their significance to adolescent female readers and their ramifications for girlhood culture at large. Plath's legacy endures in part because of the recognition that a fluctuation in moods and personas is often the experience of young women, of writers, of those who struggle with depression or anxiety (and the overlap between these populations), and also because of Plath's ability to craft the fever of her emotions into poems that rely on bold and rich figurative language. This essay uses memoir, a survey of Plath's popular and critical reception, and a close reading of Plath poems that take on more adolescent concerns and themes, then concludes by looking at contemporary women poets whose aesthetics, attitudes and themes are relevant to contemporary teenage girl readers.②

Peter J. Lowe, in "*Full Fathom Five*: The Dead Father in Sylvia Plath's Seascapes", presents a study of Sylvia Plath's use of seascapes in several of her poems. According to the author, such symbolism was her way of capturing her past happiness and dealing with her deep sense of loss over the death of her father. It cites *Full Fathom Five* and *Lorelei* where Plath uses suicidal theme as a process of reunion with his father and the beach which arouses in her that suicidal desire.③

---

① Travis I. "'I have always been Scared of You': Sylvia Plath, Perpetrator Trauma and Threatening Victims". European Journal of American Culture. 2009, 28(3):277-293.

② Greenberg A, Klaver B. "Mad Girls' Love Songs: Two Women Poets—a Professor and Graduate Student—Discuss Sylvia Plath, Angst, and the Poetics of Female Adolescence". College Literature, 2009, 36(4):179-207.

③ Lowe P J. "*Full Fathom Five*: The Dead Father in Sylvia Plath's Seascapes". Texas Studies in Literature & Language, 2007, 49(1):21-44.

Patricia Stanley, in "When Scriptotherapy Fails: The Life and Death of Sylvia Plath and Adelheid Duvanel", focuses on the factors affecting the failure on the application of scrip to therapy to recover psychic pains of American poet Sylvia Plath and Swiss writer Adelheid Duvanel. This assesses on the in effectivity of scrip to therapy or life writing for the two authors to release psychic pains, despite the fact that the method has been proven to work for memories long repressed and resolve fears. In addition, it also examines parental control and expectation as prime factors for such failure. [1]

## 2. Cultural Study

María Luisa Pascual Garrido, in "Plath's Spanish Poems and Tropes: Turning Landscape into Mindscape", argues that although critical attention has focused on Ariel, Sylvia Plath's earlier poems are also worth examining since they reveal significant details concerning the writer's evolution towards that final achievement. After getting married in June 1956, Plath and Hughes travelled to Spain and settled in Benidorm for their honeymoon. It is the poems derived from that period and Plath's response to the alien setting that are analyzed in this paper. The corpus of "Spanish poems" and its most salient motifs are identified and examined to assess the emotional and artistic response of Plath's encounter with Spain in her work. A rhetorical analysis of these poems are carried out but biographical data from Plath's journals, correspondence and prose will also be considered. Finally, two later poems are examined to demonstrate that Spain left its imprint in Plath's mind,

---

[1] Stanley P. "When Scriptotherapy Fails: The Life and Death of Sylvia Plath and Adelheid Duvanel". Seminar—A Journal of Germanic Studies, 2006, 42(4):395-411.

supplying suggestive imagery which turned the Spanish landscape into a violent mindscape.①

Renée Dowbnia, in "Consuming Appetites: Food, Sex, and Freedom in Sylvia Plath's *The Bell Jar*", presents literary criticism of the book *The Bell Jar* by Sylvia Plath. Particular focus is given to Plath's depictions of food in the novel as compared with U.S. women's magazine advertisements of the 1950s. Details on the character Esther's bulimia and its relationship to consumer capitalism are presented. Other topics include femininity, sexuality, and freedom.②

## 3. Narratology Study

Esin Kumlu, in "Not the Mad Woman in the Attic but the Cultural Critique: Understanding the Organic Writing of Sylvia Plath through *The Bell Jar*", analyzes the organic form of writing of Sylvia Plath that has been ignored by most of the Plath scholars. Although Plath achieved and maintained a unique and evolving style both in her poetry and prose, this unique style has been read under the misleading light of Plath's biography retold by different Plath scholars. Putting *The Bell Jar* at the center of the reading process, this study focuses on how Plath built an organic form of writing and also how it has been attempted by the establishment by some literary critics to remove all political connections from her entire body of work.③

---

① Garrido M L P. "Plath's Spanish Poems and Tropes: Turning Landscape into Mindscape". International Journal of English Studies, 2018, 18(2):1-17.

② Dowbnia R. "Consuming Appetites: Food, Sex, and Freedom in Sylvia Plath's *The Bell Jar*". Women's Studies, 2014, 43(5):567-588.

③ Kumlu E. "Not the Mad Woman in the Attic but the Cultural Critique: Understanding the Organic Writing of Sylvia Plath through *The Bell Jar*". Journal of Graduate School of Social Sciences, 2010, 14(2):133-145.

## 4. Biographical Study

Selma Asotić, in "Sylvia Plath and the Dangers of Biography", argues that 2013 marked the 50th anniversary of the death of Sylvia Plath and was commemorated by a flurry of new publications on the life and work of the late poet. The renewed interest in Sylvia Plath also revitalized the decades-old debate on the interdependence of her poems and her biography. This paper investigates and problematizes the way in which poetry in general and the work of Sylvia Plath in particular are read and interpreted. It tries to shed some light on the "biographical fallacy" which has for so long plagued critical approaches to her work and shows ways in which S. Plath's own poetic method differs from the method of confessional writers such as Robert Lowell, in the hope of revealing why S. Plath's work cannot and should not be approached through the prism of her biography. [1]

## 5. Eco-Criticism

Scott Knickerbocker, in "'Bodied Forth in Words': Sylvia Plath's Ecopoetics", argues that Plath demonstrates a combined interest in the texture of the natural world and the texture of language, which in her poems enacts and does not merely represent that world. Her unfortunate categorization as a "confessional" poet as well as critics' obsession with her biography have resulted in, on one hand, an underestimation of Plath's engagement with the "real world" beyond her subjectivity, and on the other hand, an insufficient consideration of the craft and

---

[1] Asotić S. "Sylvia Plath and the Dangers of Biography". Journal of Education, Culture & Society, 2015, 1:55-64.

formal properties of her poems. She was, from an early age, drawn to the natural world, although she was equally fascinated by the sounds of language. Plath's sense of irony and linguistic awareness, that is, puts her in a different category from that of a mere nature lover. Her poetry derives its power from the generative friction between speakers and a nonhuman world that resists figurative appropriation. For Plath, this resistance is itself to be figured forth, creating the formal reverberations with which her poems still startle us.[①]

## 6. Feminist Criticism

Lisa Narbeshuber, in "The Poetics of Torture: The Spectacle of Sylvia Plath's Poetry", criticizes that Sylvia Plath, in her most ambitious poems, tackles the problem of female selfhood. This desire in Plath's poetry to trace the connection between the private and the public has not been explored in any depth in Plath criticism. Instead, most criticism reads the poems *Daddy* and *Lady Lazarus* around the psychology of Plath's life, if not exclusively as biography, then as the feminist struggles of a victorious woman over a man or men. despite imagery to the contrary. The poems do not bear out the critics' assumptions. When Plath evokes images of wholeness in *Daddy* and *Lady Lazarus*, she inevitably undercuts them, emphasizing the systematic play of elements and the constructedness of meanings. She moves out of the skin of the individual and sketches out the social game, the intersubjective complexes rather than the inner strife that Judith Kroll and other Plath critics focus on. Plath de-emphasizes identity and emphasizes the roles of various systems.[②]

---

[①] Knickerbocker S. "'Bodied Forth in Words': Sylvia Plath's Ecopoetics". College Literature, 2009, 36(3):1-27.

[②] Narbeshuber L. "The Poetics of Torture: The Spectacle of Sylvia Plath's Poetry". Canadian Review of American Studies, 2004, 34(2):185-203.

## 7. New Historicism

Kathleen Spivack, in "Some Thoughts on Sylvia Plath" presents a narrative about her encounters with the poet, Sylvia Plath. During a class shared by Kathleen with Plath, sometimes she seemed restless, agitated beneath her stillness. She hardly interacted with other students. The person in class and the person revealed in Plath's letters, journals and poems were entirely different. Longing, anger, ambition, and despair appear to have been motivating factors for the poet. As in a Greek tragedy, in which the elements of destruction reside within the character of the protagonist, the elements that led to her suicide had been apparent even in the early stages of her adolescence. Her desperation increased throughout her life. Plath's favorite poet was Wallace Stevens. Her own poems were tightly controlled, formal, impenetrable, but without the feeling that was later to enter them. They did not have the passion of some of the poetry from her juvenilia; that passion had been replaced by duty and structure. Robert Lowell did not particularly praise Plath as his student, for although her poems were perfect, they had an unborn feeling to them. Plath has been celebrate, since her death, for giving voice to women's rage. [1]

---

[1] Spivack K. "Some Thoughts on Sylvia Plath". Virginia Quarterly Review, 2004, 80(2):212-218.

# Chapter 21
# Allen Ginsberg

Ginsberg was the son of Louis Ginsberg, a poet and schoolteacher in New Jersey, and of Naomi Ginsberg, a Russian Émigré, whose madness and eventual death were memorialized in *Kaddish* (1959). *Howl* combined apocalyptic criticism of the dull, prosperous Eisenhower years with exuberant celebration of an emerging counterculture. It was the best-known and most widely circulated book of poems of its time, and with its appearance Ginsberg became part of the history of publicity as well as the history of poetry. *Howl* and Jack Kerouac's novel *On the Road* (1957) were the pocket bibles of the generation whose name Kerouac had coined—"Beat", with its punning overtones of "beaten down" and "beatified". With Ginsberg's death, contemporary American poetry lost one of its most definitive and revolutionary figures. However, the poems endure.

## Critical Perspectives

## 1. New Historicism

Daniel Karlin, in "Bob Dylan and Allen Ginsberg: at Kerouac's Grave, and beyond", takes its starting point as the conversation between Allen Ginsberg and Bob Dylan at the grave of Jack Kerouac in 1975 during the Rolling Thunder Revue tour, an encounter which was filmed, photographed and narrated, both by the two artists and by others. It considers the ways in which Kerouac's work focused and mediated the friendship of Ginsberg and Dylan, their sense of each other's art, and of their own. Ginsberg's influence on Dylan was more than matched by Dylan's influence on Ginsberg, but what binds them together is an idea of American speech (whether spoken or sung) for which Kerouac is the disembodied and occluded source.[1]

Megan Tusler, in "Caption, Snapshot, Archive: On Allen Ginsberg's Photo-Poems", considers how Allen Ginsberg's process of photographing and captioning reveals a project of community formation that reconsiders the position of the social subject. For Ginsberg the documentarian, the image/caption mode is ideal for his documentary project of recording the self in relation to its community. He produces a version of the self that is relative to its community and displaces an atomized, stable self from the self-portrait. His photographs and writings show the formation of a loose cultural group and demonstrate a point of view that shows how the image/

---

[1] Karlin D. "Bob Dylan and Allen Ginsberg: at Kerouac's Grave, and beyond". Popular Music History, 2013, 8(2):155-168.

caption as medium serves as a particularly descriptive method of documenting a community's emergence. In Ginsberg's work, portraiture and self-portraiture, in particular, work to describe a loose structure of affection and desire. Picture-poems open up the possibility of seeing the group's arrangements because the aesthetic practice of cross-reading shows the photographer's investment in mimesis. Ginsberg's version of documentational aesthetics, that insists on giving durability to a historical moment, shows that he prioritizes a relation of "among", enfolding the many, instead of a relation "between" two. His archival practice, furthermore, reiterates this insistence on a documentational viewpoint that speaks to the historical moment. Ginsberg's collection, writing, photography, and arrangement insist, in contrast to the way the Beats are perceived in the press, on durability and permanence: they demonstrate a future orientation, a drive to record history. The gestural possibility of the snapshot shows its fit to capturing the ordinary and organizing the emergence of a social form.①

Luke Walker, in "Allen Ginsberg's *Wales Visitation* as a neo-Romantic Response to Wordsworth's *Tintern Abbey*", considers the 1967 visit by American Beat poet Allen Ginsberg to the Wye River Valley and the Vale of Ewyas in Wales. As a result of the trip, Ginsberg was inspired to write poetry which paid homage to English poets William Blake and William Wordsworth. The reception of Blake and Wordsworth by the American counterculture of the 1960s is explored. Poems discussed include Ginsberg's *Wales Visitation* and Wordsworth's *Lines Composed a Few Miles above Tintern Abbey*.②

---

① Tusler M. "Caption, Snapshot, Archive: On Allen Ginsberg's Photo-Poems". Criticism, 2019, 61(2):219-244.

② Walker L. "Allen Ginsberg's *Wales Visitation* as a neo-Romantic Response to Wordsworth's *Tintern Abbey*". Romanticism, 2013, 19(2):207-217.

## 2. Psychoanalytical Study

Craig Svonkin, in "Manishevitz and Sake, the Kaddish and Sutras: Allen Ginsberg's Spiritual Self-Othering", explores Allen Ginsberg's conflicted relationship to his given Jewishness. Ginsberg dealt with his ambivalence to his "endowed" identity through "transpiritualism", the adoption of marginalized spiritual identities as his own. Ginsberg's transpiritualism was quite complex, however, for he did not simply slough off an endowed Jewish identity for an appropriated or acquired Buddhist identity. Rather, Ginsberg crafted a spiritually complex, hybridized identity and thus escaped the "given" or "endowed" identity he experienced as limiting and claustrophobic. Exploring the psychological, cultural, historical, and aesthetic causes for transpiritual self-othering, Craig attempts to contextualize Ginsberg's work in the culture of 1950s America.[1]

John Tytell, in "An Emotional Time Bomb: Allen Ginsberg's *Howl* at 60", focuses on the poem *Howl* which marks its 60th anniversary in 2015. It mentions a brief background on Ginsberg and the poem that was written in San Francisco, California in 1955, the theme of the poem concerning the suffering and magnanimity aggravating the experiences of the so-called Beat Group under repression in the 1950s and assessments of the various parts of the poem which cover topics such as restraints of convention and the failure of a system.[2]

---

[1] Svonkin C. "Manishevitz and Sake, the Kaddish and Sutras: Allen Ginsberg's Spiritual Self-Othering". College Literature, 2010, 37(4):166-193.

[2] Tytell J. "An Emotional Time Bomb: Allen Ginsberg's *Howl* at 60". Antioch Review, 2015, 73(4):636-646.

## 3. Biographical Study

Jason Arthur, in "Allen Ginsberg's Biographical Gestures", discusses the editorial control of poet Allen Ginsberg to his biographies. It analyzes the text of Ginsberg's poem *The Green Automobile*, which is a period laden with identity crises brought about by the poet's academic training and his homosexuality. Mark Schechner, referring to Ginsberg's role in the publication of his journals, suggests that the poet is aware that he matters less as a poet than as a figure. It proposes that Ginsberg has always exercised an editor's control of the public side of his private life.[1]

Gary Scharnhorst, in "Moodie, My Dad, Allen Ginsberg, and Me: Reflections on Wichita and *Wichita Vortex Sutra*", describes his early years growing up in Wichita, Kansas in the 1960s. Described also is an older friend, Moodie Connell, who ran the Skidrow Beanery in downtown Wichita, and served beans, etc. to "bums & hobos" for 25 cents. Trouble developed when he invited local high school and college students to read their poetry at the Beanery. After many so-called "violations", his place was closed down and continued violations of the 1st Amendment became a typical reason for persecution and arrest of authors of that period. Allen Ginsberg's response to the *Wichita Beacon* newspaper in showed hypocrisy in treatment of writers of that period.[2]

---

[1] Arthur J. "Allen Ginsberg's Biographical Gestures". Texas Studies in Literature & Language, 2010, 52(2):227-246.

[2] Scharnhorst G. "Moodie, My Dad, Allen Ginsberg, and Me: Reflections on Wichita and *Wichita Vortex Sutra*". Midwest Quarterly, 2004, 45(4):369-380.

## 4. Cultural Study

Yaakov Ariel, in "Charisma and Counterculture: Allen Ginsberg as a Prophet for a New Generation", argues that the cultural role of Allen Ginsberg does not fit a typical Weberian model of charisma. The avant-garde poet was an outstanding personality and possessed an unusual ability to affect people. He played a vital role in expanding the boundaries of personal freedom in America of the 1950s-1990s, blazing new paths for spiritual, communal and artistic expression. Serving as a father figure for the counterculture—a symbol of an alternative set of cultural norms, lifestyles and literary forms—Ginsberg was a charismatic counter-leader, with no clearly defined followers or movement. As a leader in a more liberated era, he offered energy, ideas, inspiration, and color, but no structure or authority. Instead he was a prophet of freedom, calling on people to express themselves openly, to expand and experiment. This role demanded charisma but of a different kind—one that was more spiritual and less organizational or hierarchical. This article follows Gary Dickson's essay *Charisma, Medieval and Modern*, in offering a suggestive analysis of and supplement to Weber's understanding of charisma. The article grapples with the concept of charisma in relation to a generation that resented rigid structures and authorities. [1]

---

[1] Ariel Y. "Charisma and Counterculture: Allen Ginsberg as a Prophet for a New Generation". Religions, 2013, 4(1):51-66.